CW01498080

WHAT WITCHES WANT

WITCHING HOUR
BOOK 7

CHRISTINE ZANE THOMAS

1

SECRETS

DAVE

Some secrets—most secrets—have a short shelf-life. They're held behind sealed lips for the briefest moment before being uttered then passed along.

Some secrets have staying power. They're kept for weeks, for months, sometimes years. But eventually, the thing that's hidden finds its way out.

Then there's the *other* type of secret. A secret meant to go to the grave. Meant to be buried deep—so deep the only way to find it is to dig from the *other* side.

I had one of those secrets.

2

CONSTANCE CAMPBELL AND THE CURSED MOON

I whispered a curse up at the moon.

Not a witchy curse. There was no magic involved. Just a string of bad words. Seven, to be exact. And they were strung together in an order I doubted the moon had ever heard before—not even uttered by the saltiest of sailors.

The funny thing was, the moon wasn't even there. It hid behind the clouds somewhere above me in a vast wintery sky.

It was an unseasonably warm January night in Creel Creek, Virginia. Here, in the foothills of the Blue Ridge Mountains, the sky was overcast, despite the forecast being clear with no chance of rain or snow.

In fact, the weather was nice enough for Dave's youngest girls, Elsie and Kacie, to request we make a fire in the backyard fire pit.

We, meaning my mother and me. Mom hadn't told the girls no since the moment she met them, several months ago. She wasn't going to start tonight.

Neither was I. Tonight was hard enough.

So, with the moon hidden above us, we roasted marshmallows. The girls drank copious amounts of hot chocolate against the crisp, but not cold, night air.

Kacie, who was only three when Dave and I started dating, was now in the second grade. With her dark hair and big brown eyes, she reminded me of her father. She stuffed what had to be her eighth s'more into her mouth.

Beside her, with a mouth equally full of the campfire treat, Dave's middle child grinned. Elsie's cheeks were streaked with chocolate and her lips covered in crumbs. Unlike the other two, Elsie's hair was lighter. She favored their mother except she had Dave's nose and thin lips.

"What do you think, girls?" Mom asked them. "Are we about ready to go inside?"

"One more!" Kacie pleaded.

It was already well past their bedtime. But again, the night was hard enough without forcing them to go to bed.

"How many is that?" I asked, then added, "You're going to give yourself a tummy ache."

"I already have one," she said flatly. "But I can't stop eating. They're so good!"

"So good!" Elsie agreed. "Please, Constance!"

I gave them a look—a look meant to say there was no chance of another s'more.

"Please!" Kacie clasped her hands together.

I had no resolve. Not tonight. "All right. One more. Just remember, your tummy aches are your own fault."

It didn't help when my mother came to their aid. "Tummy aches?" she scoffed. "You're not allowed to get a tummy ache when Nana Serena's around."

"Really, Mom?"

"What? If my magic happens to cure them, well, that's

because I can't control it as well as I used to." She winked at me, then loaded another marshmallow on Elsie's stick.

"My tummy's already better." Kacie beamed.

"Mine's not." Elsie gazed up expectantly at my mother.

My beautiful mother didn't disappoint. She handed Elsie the stick, scrunched her mouth in a ball, and thought a moment.

"Let's see," she said. "What's the spell to cure tummy aches? Ah, yes. I think I've got it.

"There's no cookie you can bake, that'll cure a little tummy ache.
But in magic, I always find, a cure that's one-of-a-kind.
A hiccup will ease the pain. A burp might help the strain.
But it's the toots that'll make it disappear.
Therefore, you have nothing to fear from a little stomachache, my dear."

I snorted a laugh. "So, if they fart, their stomachache goes away?"

"The best I could think of." Mom shrugged unapologetically. "What do you say, girls? Did it work?"

Elsie bent to the side. "It works!"

A silent and deadly smell wafted in my direction.

"A. Gross. B. Does Nana Serena spoil you or what?"

The little girl hovered the marshmallow over the flame. A moment later, there was no hint of trepidation as she devoured another s'more.

"Nana Serena doesn't spoil us *that* much," she said, chewing.

"You only spoil us when Daddy's gone," Kacie added.

"Wait. I spoil you?" I smiled. "Are you sure?"

Both girls nodded.

Mom set Kacie up with another marshmallow, which she thrust straight into the flame. It crackled, glowing red hot before turning jet black.

It was still burning when she yanked it out of the fire. She blew it out with a giant breath like birthday candles on a cake. "Allie's going to be jealous when we tell her about this."

At the mention of Allie's name, my stomach lurched. I pictured Dave's oldest daughter at the dining room table that morning. She ate waffles and tuned out Dave as he tried, for what had to be the hundredth time, to lecture her before they headed off for a campsite deep in the mountains.

For her sisters, Allie had feigned excitement. She put on a brave face. But there were other emotions hidden behind her moody teenage facade. Plus, she'd been acting out for weeks. Dave blamed hormones. I knew better.

It didn't matter how long she'd known this day would come. It was simple. The notion of shifting into a werewolf for the first time scared her. Although she wouldn't admit that to Dave.

I just wished her Aunt Imogene was here. A few months ago, Dave's sister, her husband Jared, and their two boys had moved across the country for Jared's job.

Imogene would've stepped in. She would've known exactly what to say to ease Allie's transition.

Not being a werewolf myself, I didn't feel it was my place to say anything to her or to Dave. Now, I was thinking otherwise.

"She won't be jealous," Elsie told her sister. "You know, I bet she won't even like sweets anymore. She'll be craving red meat when she gets back."

"Yuck!" Kacie's mouth contorted. "If that's true, I don't want to become a wolf."

"It's not true," I said. "Do you think your dad could live in a world without ice cream? Without chocolate cake?"

"No." She narrowed her eyes at Elsie. "Why do you always have to tease me?"

"I wasn't teasing. She really will crave red meat. Right, Constance?"

I sighed. "I think we should wait and see what Allie's like when she gets back. And maybe give her space. I highly doubt her eating habits will change."

"I hope not," Kacie said, eyeing the stack of Hershey bars beside the fire. "I love sweets. I love chocolate."

"Dogs can't have chocolate." This time, Elsie was teasing.

The girls bickered back and forth before finally settling down a few minutes later. They whispered to each other, staring up at the clouds. Still, the moon was nowhere to be found.

I cursed it again anyway.

In my mind, the moon was a villain.

Although, it hadn't always been. I could remember a night when I was little, riding in the back of my parents' Jeep Wagoneer. From the front seat, my mother turned, and she pointed out my window. Mom told me about the moon and the stars—about the patterns they wove around our world.

She said every full moon had a name. There was the Harvest Moon of the fall equinox, her personal favorite, and the Hunter's Moon in October. Then there was the Cold Moon of December.

It made sense. Before the calendar, it was the phases of the moon that guided our ancestors from season to season. The moon was like a giant clock face in the sky. It ensured they planted seeds in time for harvest, and they were well stocked for the harsh winter ahead.

Mom had disappeared not long after that night.

I had very few memories of my mother from my childhood. Those I did have, I held onto tightly. Kind of like how my dad held onto the Wagoneer. It had sat in our garage long after the engine stopped running.

Eventually, he let it go. He sold it to some guy who came over and towed it away.

I couldn't do the same with the moon. It was always up there. A constant. A reminder that my mother was gone.

She wasn't there to raise me—to remind me the names of the moons. To watch over me as I transitioned into womanhood. Nor was she there when I became something else entirely.

A witch.

At the age of forty, I became a witch. It was then I learned my mother had been part of a secret magical organization known as the Faction. Her disappearance happened while on a mission for them.

This new knowledge ate at me. I made it my mission to find my mother and bring down whoever was responsible for taking her away from me.

With the help of a few friends, my grandmother, and a celestial being or two—demonic and otherwise—I was able to return my mother's spirit to her body.

But it didn't end there.

Mom wasn't herself. She'd been enchanted by a warlock, a man impersonating a wizard. And someone I thought of as a friend. Someone who claimed to be part of the Faction when in reality the organization was a construct of his design, made so he could toy with the paranormal world.

Ivan Rush was a liar and a thief of the worst kind. He

was a soul stealer. For years, he used the Faction to lure witches into traps. He stole their magic. He stole their *secrets*. He made deals with devils—literally releasing demons into our world.

The Faction made it so Ivan could keep those who would oppose him underneath his thumb.

With all his planning—his scheming—Ivan thought he'd accounted for everything.

He was wrong.

The warlock wasn't expecting Jezebel Young and Serena Campbell.

Gran and Mom trapped Ivan in a demon's realm. Unfortunately, this trap came at a great cost. For Mom, her body— her spirit trapped in the body of an owl. For Gran, she lost her memory of what happened to her daughter.

When Ivan was eventually set free, he set his sights on me. Another mistake. Again, Ivan lost.

Except it didn't feel exactly like a win. Not to me. Because Ivan got away.

I stared into the eyes of the woman who ultimately caused his downfall. Mom's piercing blue eyes were nearly the same shade as mine. And though her blonde hair held a few more grays than mine, it was straighter. It obeyed her styling commands as if by magic.

Looking at her was like looking into a futuristic mirror.

No, Mom hadn't been there when I turned forty and became a witch. Nor was she there for the big moments. My marriage. My divorce. She wasn't there for me when my dad died either. She didn't see its aftermath—when I had to fight the demon that killed him.

But thanks to a clever spell, a note written on the spelled page of a spelled book, Mom remembered everything—her childhood with Gran, their falling out, and their reconciliation. She remembered me as a little girl. She even had flashes of memories from the time she was the owl.

I spent so long searching for her and tracking down the spell to make her better. A part of me thought it was over.

Another part of me knew it wasn't. Not yet. Not with Ivan still out there.

But that was a matter for another time.

What mattered now was she was here. These past few months meant everything to me. Us being together made my heart full and happy.

Across the fire, Mom eyed me as if she knew what I was thinking. "What has you so deep in thought?" she asked softly, so the girls couldn't hear.

"The moon," I said.

It wasn't a lie. If losing her had strained my relationship with our celestial neighbor, then falling in love with a were-wolf had dealt the final blow. Our ancestors might've looked at the moon like it was a clock. To me, it was a ticking time bomb. I didn't think I could hate it any more than I already did. Not until today. Not until I saw the trepidation all over Allie's sweet face.

"She's going to be all right," Mom said. "It's in her blood."

"That's the problem," I whispered. "It's a curse, and it's in her blood."

The moon seemed to resent my wording. Overhead, the Wolf Moon tore through the clouds like the knee on my favorite pair of jeans.

With a red blanket wrapped around her shoulders, Mom held a cup of hot chocolate to her lips. She sighed into it, not really knowing what to say. It didn't matter. Words were hardly necessary when it came to her magic.

I felt a wave of energy brush over me.

I fiddled with the frayed ends of those jeans. It was getting late. The girls were quiet. The only sound was the crackling of the fire. I felt warm and comforted. My eyelids were heavy. One moment, I was staring into the fire, and the next I was nodding off.

My eyes closed, and just as I was falling to sleep, something let out a howl in the distance.

3

A MIDWINTER NIGHT'S NOT-A-DREAM

The breeze isn't cold. Not even remotely. But still, it sets my teeth on edge. I fight chills down my body, through my shoulders and chest. My legs tense. My spine goes rigid. For some reason, I'm expecting this. Part of me wants this to happen.

There's something inside me, and it's ready to get out.

I can feel it—like it's waiting for something. What, I don't know.

It should happen any time now, a release of some sort. I feel as if it's about to be set free.

But it's not. I'm still here, and I'm shivering, alone in the dark.

It takes a moment, but I realize why I'm shivering. It's because I'm naked. Even though the temperature's above freezing, there are parts of me that never like to be exposed to Mother Nature.

And that's where I seem to be. In Mother Nature.

I wish the world would come into focus. It's pitch black all around me. I can't see more than a few feet ahead. There's a canopy of trees above me. The ground is wet. The air smells woodsy—of ozone and dead leaves. There's a fire somewhere in the distance.

I'm somewhere in the woods, only I don't remember setting a foot in them. I don't remember how I got here or why.

There is a reason for it, I can sense that, but it's just out of reach, even as I stretch my mind to the brink.

My mind—that's another problem. My head is throbbing with a dull pain. My heart beats loudly in my chest. And my skin is itching with discomfort.

This feels wrong. So wrong. But I can't figure out why, at least not aside from the obvious.

I'm in the middle of nowhere. I'm naked. And I'm alone.

Or at least I think I'm alone.

There's a rustle in the shrubbery behind me, a snapping of twigs. Then something howls—actually howls—long and piercing. I flinch. Whatever it is, it's too close for comfort.

The rustling gets louder. Something is getting closer. I can hear its ragged breaths. I can sense its menacing presence.

I run but it's too dark to see. I don't know where I'm running to, just away—away from this thing that keeps getting nearer.

I'm in trouble, and I'm pretty sure it's too late to call for help.

I run faster, but my feet lose their grip on the slippery ground. I slide through some underbrush and nearly tumble down a hill. I right myself, but it's only for a moment. The thing, whatever it is, is on me now. I'm sure it has me.

I make a last-ditch effort to get away. I rocket down the hill, half running, half rolling, and just hoping I won't break any bones or get gashed by any rocks as I go down, down, down.

I crash to the bottom of the hill and lie still. I'm sprawled on my back, gasping for breath.

Above me, the moon is just visible behind the clouds. Part of me thanks the heavens for this while another holds the moon accountable for every wrong I've ever been dealt.

I'm confused as to why these parts of me are so conflicted, but I don't have time to piece together the whys because the thing—the monster—is back. And its angry growls seem to surround me.

The beast lets out another howl just before the darkness caves in around me.

4

IN WITCH IT'S TIME FOR A BEDTIME STORY

I jerked awake, feeling as if I'd just fallen down a mountainside. In truth, I hadn't even fallen out of my chair. I was, however, slumped over with my head lolled sideways. With the back of my hand, I swiped away some chocolatey drool that was running down my cheek.

Groggily, I asked Mom, "Did your spell just put me to sleep?"

"I don't think so," she said, unsure. "At least it wasn't meant to. I was just hoping you'd relax a little."

"Well, I did and then some. How long was I out?"

"Not long." Mom's smile was as wide as ever. "In fact, I was about to wake you up. You were dreaming like a little puppy, making all sorts of noises."

I wanted to laugh but found it difficult. Mom was right. There had been a dream, but I couldn't remember what it had been about. Whatever it was left me with a sense of hovering dread.

"Is everything okay with you and Dave?" Mom asked. "It sounded like you said his name once or twice. You know, sometimes our dreams tell us more than we want to know about what's going on inside our head."

"Thanks to you, I know more about dreams and their magical connection to our mind than I ever wanted to know."

"That doesn't answer my question."

"We're fine."

It was the truth. There was nothing wrong with me and Dave. At least not *my* Dave. It was the *other* guy that was the problem.

Nights like this, with Dave—and now Allie—gone were hard.

On cue, something howled in the distance. It wasn't a wolf. And definitely not a werewolf. Despite knowing it had to be a neighbor's dog, a chill ran down my spine.

"You're sure everything's fine?"

"I didn't say everything's fine."

"Good. Cause I wouldn't believe you if you had." Mom leaned back in her chair.

Again, I tried to coax the dream out, but nothing came. It was almost like it wasn't my dream at all. The sense of dread wouldn't leave. The hairs on my neck stayed prickled.

Surely, that means nothing too.

I blamed the moon, which had finally clawed through the clouds. It was now full and bright above us. With a full moon, there always seemed to be a hint of danger in the air. Perhaps because more often than not, there was.

There were plenty of things to be afraid of. Paranormal things. Vampires. Demons. Then there were the hunters of various varieties. In just a few years, I'd run into everything at least once. They all liked to poke their heads out when the moon was at its brightest.

Ivan Rush was still out there. He was the enemy. He

knew when Dave was gone, I was at my most vulnerable—in more ways than one.

There were little girls to protect.

Across the fire, Elsie's eyelids were droopy as she stroked Licorice across the back. The black cat had curled itself into a ball in her lap.

Beside them, Kacie was down for the count. Fast asleep, she cuddled against her sister's shoulder. Both girls still had chocolate smeared across their cheeks. A problem for another time.

Mom looked to be in hog heaven. Her eyes followed mine to her would-be grandchildren. That was if Dave and I ever made things official.

Another problem for another time.

I didn't know if it was the lingering effects of Mom's spell or just the weight of the day hitting me, but I was as tired as the girls. Ready to curl up under the covers and wait for morning.

Maybe tonight I could do just that with my eyes closed. With Dave gone, a restful night's sleep was the exception, not the rule.

Mom let out a sigh and nodded toward Kacie. "I'll take her if you'll get the other."

"Sure thing." With the wave of a hand and a magic word, I put out the fire.

Elsie didn't protest as I scooped her up. She went limp before we made it up the stairs to the room they shared.

With the girls in bed, we aimed to do the same ourselves, but not before we convened for yet another night-time ritual.

For the time being, Mom had taken the guest bedroom —what used to be Dave's office. His old basketball trophies and other junk were moved to the garage. We'd shoved his desk into the corner of the room and fit a full-size bed in the center with a small bookshelf and a nightstand.

Now that Mom had gone through almost everything the TV had to offer, she'd started in on a pile of romance novels —most of it, the spillover from the bookstore. There was a stack on the nightstand. She put a cup of water next to the books, then grabbed an old one from the shelf.

This book wasn't like the others. While they were all used, with tattered covers and yellowed pages, this book was even older. Its leather cover was torn. Its binding hung on by threads. It was our family grimoire.

Setting it between us on the bed, she flipped it open to the very last page.

"What do you want to know tonight?"

Stretching into a yawn, I pondered the question. What did I want to know? What story hadn't already been told?

This nighttime routine was my idea—a way for us to get to know each other again after so many years apart. The whole thing was a little silly, a little self-serving, but a lot of fun.

The way it worked was I asked a question. Mom answered. She told a story. It didn't have to be about magic, but the subject was typically broached.

That was where the book came into play. Our family grimoire held many things, from private spells to potion recipes and more. But most of all, the book traced our family's lineage from its early witchy beginnings to Gran's exploits as a witch, serving as a nurse during the Korean War. It chronicled her meeting my grandfather, his tragic death, and her moving to Creel Creek to start fresh where her ancestors had once lived.

There was even mention of the magical mine, now destroyed thanks to me.

Where the book was lacking began right around the time of my mother's disappearance. It was as if Gran had forgotten to keep up with it. Or maybe she just didn't have the heart to try.

We were trying to fill in the gaps.

The grimoire did the heavy lifting. It listened, jotting down the parts it deemed important, leaving out the fluff.

The way Mom told things, there was a lot of fluff. Whether it was because of my spell or because she spent so long without a memory, Mom's ability to recall the tiniest details was now heightened.

Unfortunately, it sent the book into fits.

I wasn't helping. The book drummed its front and back cover like a person might drum their fingers with anxious impatience.

"Okay. I'm thinking. How 'bout you tell me how you met Dad."

Mom's eyebrows knitted. "He never told you?"

"He did, but I've never heard it from your perspective."

The book flapped its pages in a sigh.

"Aw! He's mad there's no magic in this one."

"Not exactly true," Mom said.

My eyebrows took on a similar shape. "But you weren't forty. He told me y'all met in college on an ultimate frisbee team."

"Well"—she winced—"that part is true. He was so athletic back then. Strong and handsome. Plus, he was damn good with a flick."

"Mom!"

"What? That's what it's called when you throw a frisbee. What'd you think I meant?"

I opened my mouth to tell her but thought better. "Never mind."

"It wasn't something sexual, was it?"

I grimaced into a laugh. "Tell me about the magic. I know you weren't a witch."

"Not yet. But unlike you, I knew magic existed. I couldn't perform spells yet, but I could sense when there was magic around. And I knew how to bend the rules a little.

"I recruited other paranormals for the team. There was a girl who was part harpy. She didn't know it, but had she believed, she would've been able to fly. I'm sure it also accounted for her nasty attitude. But she could catch anything thrown her way. Then there was this guy who I don't know what he was, but he was speedy. Your dad— there was something about him too."

"So, you recruited him and y'all hit it off?"

"No. Your dad was shy. I don't think we even talked outside of ultimate."

"Then how'd you start dating?"

"What'd he tell you?"

"He said y'all hit it off at a party after the league championship or whatever."

"Somewhat true," Mom said. "But this is the part of the story he wouldn't know. I never told him. I was afraid he'd see things differently than I did."

I got comfortable on the mattress. "How so?"

"Well," she started. "There was someone else on the team. A seer named Maisie Saxon. She was my roommate and one of my best friends. You know, I'd say I should call her, but you'd imagine she'd know I'm back, right?"

"You still might want to call her," I said, smiling. "How does Maisie factor in?"

Mom's smile turned sheepish. "One night, we were a little tipsy and a lot stupid. I talked her into offering the whole floor a reading—including me."

"And?"

"And she saw him. Us. Me with your father. Except it was years down the road. Honey, I don't know if what I did changed our fates. Or if maybe it was always meant to be like this."

"You asked him out?"

She shook her head. "No, but I made that party happen. And I made sure he 'accidentally' walked in on me changing in our room."

"You didn't!"

"He only saw my bra." She rolled her eyes.

The book let out a groan as it slammed shut.

———

A FEW MINUTES LATER, I curled up in my own bed—the bed I shared with Dave. Except Dave wasn't there. I put my feet in his empty spot and pictured him complaining about their temperature or lack thereof. Funny because he never dared to push them away. If anything, he'd scoot closer.

Tonight, his spot was as cold as my feet.

I lay there wishing I were as tired as I'd been outside. I contemplated using a spell. But magic worked on need, not desire. I doubted the spell would even work.

I hadn't been in bed long when headlights brightened the window shades. It wasn't necessarily an uncommon occurrence. Dave's house was located at the end of the street where a cul-de-sac allowed cars to turn around, if needed. Typically, some headlights would briefly shine into the window, then we'd hear the car speed off the other direction.

These stayed put, bright lights piercing the shades and illuminating the bedroom with eerie artificial light.

Outside, a car door slammed, sending another chill shot down my spine.

This time, I couldn't ignore it. Witchy energy flew to my fingertips.

The need was there.

I shot up from bed, crept to the window, then peeked through a crack in the shades. An SUV sat idling at the edge of the driveway. Its headlights made it impossible to make out its color or model.

That was weird. Not good.

More pressing, there was a man just ahead of it, cloaked like a shadow in the middle of the beams. He was staggering up the driveway toward the house.

He looked out of it. Drunk or maybe impaired in some *other* way.

I raced down the stairs and realized halfway down that I didn't even bring my phone. I couldn't call 9-1-1. I was afraid to yell out for Mom, for fear of waking the girls.

Maybe this was nothing.

Maybe he had the wrong house.

My eye found the peephole on the front door, and I stared out. My heartbeat picked up speed.

I watched as the man stumbled from the driveway in the direction of the sidewalk, but he doubled over into the grass.

Who is he?

Why is he here?

Part of me thought he could be a hunter—a man bent on ridding the world of werewolves, vampires, and other para-normal kind.

I pushed the notion away. It didn't make any sense. Whoever he was, he was obviously hurt.

Should I help him?

Opening the door seemed like a dumb move. After all, I

wasn't home alone. There were three other people counting on me for their protection.

But he's hurt. He could be dying.

Staying put, yelling up to Mom, and calling the police was the obvious choice.

I unbolted the door.

You're so, so dumb, Constance Campbell.

Barefoot, I ran out into the yard, unsure who or what I might find. Magical energy coursed into my fingertips. I readied a spell that would knock whoever this was on his ass —that was, of course, had he not already been there.

The man lay sprawled on the grass, his chest heaving long, ragged breaths. He was shirtless and shoeless. He wore a pair of jeans, but they weren't even buttoned at the top, just zipped, as if he'd put them on in quite a hurry. And all of him was covered in something that looked an awful lot like blood.

My heart stopped.

It was Dave.

"Oh, no." I rushed over to him. "You're hurt."

"I'm not hurt." He sucked in a heavy, ragged breath. "Not... not really."

I would've laughed, but it wasn't funny. I couldn't help but point out the obvious. "Dave," I said. "You're covered in blood."

"Right, this." He smeared a hand across his blood-drenched chest, then hovered it above his face and stared up at his palm. "This *isn't* my blood."

5

CONSTANCE CAMPBELL AND THE BLOODY BOYFRIEND

"What do you mean it's not your blood?"

For a moment, it looked like Dave might answer. He opened his mouth and puffed out a small breath, but the words didn't come. Dave's eyelids closed.

"Dave!" I shook him awake, magic flowing through my fingertips into him. Those eyes fluttered open once more. But Dave's stare was vacant.

Something was dreadfully wrong.

My heart raced, and my mind pinged from one problem to the next. I had to get to a phone. I had to call for help.

While my main concern was the blood covering his hands and chest, there was something else niggling at the back of my mind—something more deeply concerning. I just couldn't quite place what it was.

Not until I looked up and found the moon. The godforsaken moon. The moon I'd shot a curse at no less than an hour before.

The problem got a whole lot bigger.

Dave was Dave—plain old, ordinary Dave—when he

should've been the wolf. He wasn't supposed to be here in Creel Creek. He was supposed to be in the mountains with Allie, and she was nowhere to be found.

Or at least Allie wasn't perched in the front seat of his Interceptor—the souped-up Ford Explorer with the word SHERIFF wrapped along the side. It was still idling ahead of the driveway, its headlights beaming into the garage.

Dave's eyes closed again. This time, I couldn't shake him hard enough—or I couldn't mix enough magic to force him awake once more.

Mom! I mixed the magic coursing in my veins with a silent plea, hoping she might hear it and wake up. I needed help.

I needed someone's help.

My familiar Brad could read my thoughts. But our relationship status would be listed as "it's complicated" on social media.

Mom made her presence known with a cough. Then she sent her own magical thoughts unfiltered into my head.

Is that Dave?

What happened to him?

Shouldn't he be a wolf?

I was just about asleep too. Now I'll never be able to—

"Just get out here," I called in a low voice.

Barefoot, Mom tiptoed out into the grass.

"I don't think he's dead." She motioned at his rib cage which rose and fell. "And you never told me he has a six pack."

"Mom!"

"Sorry," she said. "I was never good in situations like this. I wish your Gran were here. She'd know what to do. What do you need?"

"Help?" I shrugged. "I don't know."

"Right. All that blood—it doesn't exactly look healthy."

"Yeah, well, he says it's not his blood."

"So, you talked to him?"

I nodded. "Not really. He passed out as soon as I got out here. Maybe we should get him a doctor or something."

"I'm thinking 'or something' sounds best." Mom grimaced. "What would happen if he suddenly turned? He might rip a doctor's throat out."

"True." I nodded along. "But there is a doctor at the hospital who's werewolf sympathetic. He treated Dave when he got shot a few years ago. We could call him."

"We should do that." Mom craned her neck from side to side. "But first I think we should get him inside. I have a funny feeling we're being watched."

It turned out, we were.

The trimmed bushes between the sidewalk and driveway came to life, rustling as the chubby figure of a raccoon scampered between us and the door. His booming voice echoed in both our heads. "She's right. You should get him inside. He's not safe out here in the moonlight."

I stooped beside Dave to get him up, expecting Mom to do the same, but she just stood there, mouth agape. She looked half-terrified.

Then I understood why—Dave's eyes had opened. They stared blankly at the moon above.

"Careful, Constance," Mom warned.

"It's fine. He's fine."

"He's really not," Brad said.

I ignored him.

"Dave"—my words came out shaky—"whose blood is this?"

A part of me already seemed to know.

"It's... it's Allie's," he said, breathless. "It's Allie's blood. But it's fine—she's fine."

Brad's raccoon-self growled. "You humans should stop saying things are fine when they are so obviously not."

He was right. I couldn't imagine how Dave's words could be true. There was so much blood. His arms and his chest were covered in it. It was Allie's blood. She was hurt. And she was alone.

"Is that—" Dave struggled to his feet.

"It's Brad," I told him. And since Dave couldn't speak familiar and hadn't understood Brad's growl, I said, "He says you're not safe here in the yard."

"I'm all right," Dave argued. "Just winded."

Despite the protest, he staggered toward the door. He took two steps, then fell to his knees. I caught one side of him before he face-planted, but the slick blood on his chest made it hard to keep a hold on him. He nearly brought me down with him before Mom slid beneath his other arm.

We carried him inside.

Brad followed.

"You're inviting this thing in, too?" Dave slurred. His speech was hardly coherent now.

"This thing?" Brad sneered. "Tell him *this thing* is going to save his life."

EXCEPT I COULDN'T TELL Dave how Brad was going to save his life because as soon as we dragged him inside, Dave passed out... again.

We dropped his limp body next to the living room couch. The blood made streaks on the hardwood floor, and somehow it had splattered on the walls and off-white couch. The whole place looked like a crime scene.

Who am I kidding—it probably is a crime scene.

More than anything, I wanted to know what had happened out there and if Allie was okay.

One thing at a time.

"I'll get my phone," I said.

No one else had rushed to the rescue. Mom had started cleaning the floor, as if that mattered now.

Brad clambered onto the couch to put himself at eye level.

"You don't need your phone," he said. "I know what this is."

I arched a brow. "You do?"

"He has moon poisoning. It's what happens when a werewolf doesn't turn, and then they're exposed to the moonlight."

"But why didn't he turn?" I asked.

Brad threw up his paws. "How should I know?"

"I thought maybe you saw something."

"Saw something?" Brad scoffed. "Heavens no. I was partaking in your leftovers when I heard the commotion out front."

"Leftovers?" Mom looked up. "I thought I cleaned up."

"You did." Brad's eyes narrowed. "I had to dig in the trash. Again. You know I love s'mores, right? Thanks for the invite."

"You could've invited yourself," I said. "It wouldn't've been the first time."

"I thought about it. But the cat doesn't like me. Something about not wanting to share a food bowl. Go figure."

"Can we worry about your food woes some other time?"

Mom sprayed cleaner on the floor. "I'm still trying to figure out how a werewolf doesn't turn at the full moon."

"There are several ways," I said.

Dave let out a snore, as if he could hear us.

"Okay, well, at least a few."

I didn't have first-hand experience with any of them. My knowledge was built on brief conversations with Dave.

"Like?" Mom wiped the floor, then she scooted over next to Dave. She checked his pulse like she was a nurse.

"Like he could've been shot with silver," I said. "That would explain the blood."

"Except," Brad boomed, "this isn't his blood. He said so."

"Sure, that's what he said. But he wasn't exactly coherent, was he?"

"And his pulse is fine," Mom added.

I searched for a wound of some kind. As expected, there wasn't anything to be found on his torso. No holes through his arm or neck.

I began to clean him off like Mom had done the floor—minus the chemical cleaner. "I guess this really is Allie's blood. I wish he'd told us what happened."

"He will," Mom said. "That is, once Brad tells us how to fix him."

"Oh, that." Brad's tone mellowed. "It's easy enough. Constance, do you remember the daylight potion—the one that killed your vampire boss?"

"How could I forget?" With some side effects—and lethal to vampires—the daylight potion was a way for a werewolf to avoid their rendezvous with the moon.

"He'll need a dose of its antidote, so to speak," Brad said. "And the sooner the better. Otherwise, tonight's exposure might knock him out for several days."

"Antidote?"

"Same potion," Mom said, "but stirred the opposite direction."

I shook my head. This wasn't going to be as easy as Brad was leading on. "That's a complicated potion. It must be brewed at a certain phase of the moon—"

"This phase," Brad said. "The full moon."

"Right. But it's not like we have the ingredients on hand."

"You might." Brad's beady eyes narrowed on my mother.

She winced. "What are they?"

"Mom... is there something you need to tell me?"

Brad could read Mom's mind. And mine too. But I couldn't see whatever he'd seen. I needed her to talk.

"Please don't be mad at me." She cringed. "I didn't know what she wanted them for. I thought maybe it was for a love potion or—I don't know. Something else. Not this."

"You mean Allie did this?" I guessed.

Mom nodded. "And I'm guessing he must've taken it on accident."

"But that still doesn't explain what happened to her. Or if she's all right."

"Then you two better get to potion making," Brad said.

Luckily, Mom had enough of the ingredients lying around for us to brew a small dosage of antidote. And since we were able to do so around midnight—the witching hour —the potion's effect was nearly instantaneous.

I splashed a mouthful on his tongue, clasped his mouth shut, and forced him to swallow. Within a second, he bolted upright.

For a moment, I thought the wolf might make an appearance. It seemed like he did too. His eyes went wild. He bared his teeth. Then he snarled, "Where is she?"

"It's okay." I put a reassuring hand on his still sticky shoulder. "You're better now. Or you will be."

I helped Dave sit up and handed him a cup of brownish liquid. "Drink the rest."

He peered down at it warily. "I'm guessing this isn't kombucha."

He forced down the rest as Mom and I cleaned up the mess we'd made. Containing the sludgy potion inside the cauldron had proven difficult. There were flecks of brownish ooze on the walls. Perhaps we should've used the stove instead of the living room fireplace, as Brad had so helpfully pointed out after the fact.

I'd wanted to stay close to Dave anyway.

What amazed me most was that neither of the girls woke up while we brewed and chanted. Kids really can sleep through anything.

I watched as Mom spelled away the red from the couch.

I tried to use one of my own spells, but the magic didn't deem it necessary. So, I began to scrub the wall.

Cup in hand, Dave got up. He made it a whole two feet to the couch where he laid a wary eye on Brad, still perched atop a pillow. Deciding not to fight the familiar's presence, Dave took a seat at the other end.

Mom huffed.

All that cleaning for naught.

"So, what happened?" Dave asked.

I holstered my sponge. "We were kind of hoping you'd tell us."

Dave struggled a moment, taking everything in—the wrecked living room with a cauldron taking up space under the mantle, his tattered pants and the blood still staining them, then finally the cup in his hand. "Do I really have to drink this? It's a potion, isn't it?"

Mom nodded.

"This will be the second time tonight. Neither by

choice." He grimaced and downed the liquid—if it could be called that. Taking a potion wasn't like drinking a nasty drink—although it was that too. There were other—literal —elements at play.

Wind, water, fire, and earth combined with the magic to make Dave's chest heave, his pale face go red, and his eyes close in painful discomfort. It was over in a flash. He stuck his tongue out like he'd just taken the world's worst shot of alcohol.

Mom snorted a laugh. "Now can you tell us what happened? How did you end up with Allie's potion?"

He sighed. "You know I can be a little on the suspicious side of things—what can I say? I'm a creature of habit. But I never—and I mean never—would've expected Allie to do something like this. I'm guessing I have one of you to thank for it."

His eyes lingered on Mom.

"I didn't know," she said meekly. "And you're good as new, aren't you?"

"Right." He barked a laugh. "No harm. No foul."

"What about Allie?" Dave's lackadaisical attitude put me on edge. I wanted to know what happened. "Is she okay?"

"She's fine," he said.

"You're sure?"

He nodded, and my heart finally settled into a more reasonable rhythm.

"So, she didn't take the potion," Mom said.

Dave continued his nod.

"No. And I don't think she was going to. This was just a big misunderstanding. My fault really. I should've left well enough alone. But not me. I can't let things go. I should've trusted her."

"She made a potion, Dave. What do you mean you should've trusted her?"

"Yeah, well, you know how she's been lately. So moody. She wasn't talking to me out there. She carried this bottle up to the campsite with her, and she kept staring at it. I tried to lighten the mood. I asked her if it was kombucha. She says, 'Dad, does it matter? You hate that stuff.' And boy was she right. It tasted awful."

"It wasn't kombucha," Mom pointed out.

"Funny, I'm beginning to realize that now." He smiled. "Anyway, we split up. I tried to give her some privacy, some space to make the change. Being a teenage girl and all, I didn't figure she'd want to—"

"We get the picture," I said.

"I thought you might." He smiled again.

"Then what happened?" Mom asked.

"That's where things get a little fuzzy. I was standing there, waiting—waiting for it to happen. It felt like it always does. Like there's electricity in the air. I'm not sure if it's anticipation or what, but my senses heighten. And they did for a second. But then, nothing."

"Nothing?" Mom and I both repeated.

"Nothing," he chorused again. "Just didn't happen. Not for me at least. It did for her. I heard a howl and knew things were not going in the right way. I made a break for the campsite, but she tracked me down before I got there."

"Allie attacked you?"

Dave nodded slowly.

My heart began to amp up again. Something about his story rang a bell. It was familiar. I just couldn't place why.

"Then what?" Mom leaned closer.

"Then I had to scare her away. My own daughter." He shook his head. "I used a tree limb at first. Took a few swipes at her. She hadn't really got her feet yet. And I got lucky. When I made it to the campsite, I got the gun."

"You mean he shot her?" Brad made himself known in my head.

"Dave, you didn't..."

"She's fine," he reiterated. "She's a werewolf, and this wasn't a silver bullet. She'll heal. Hell, I'm sure she already has."

"But you don't know it."

"Constance," he said softly. "I've been a werewolf my whole damn life. I've made this change every full moon for nearly thirty years. I've been shot, accidentally and on purpose. I think I know a little more about it than you."

"Fair," I said, but I thought the opposite.

In truth, Dave didn't know if Allie was okay. She was out there alone, possibly hurt, and he couldn't protect her.

"Trust me," he said. "We'll go out tomorrow morning. We'll find her. I doubt she's too far from camp. And I swear to you, nothing bad will have happened."

6

DAVE MARSTERS AND THE SLIP OF A TONGUE

Dave awoke before the sun and stood beside the bed. I wasn't sure he got any sleep. Granted, I hadn't either.

I managed maybe an hour or two, but I kept waking up throughout the night wondering what Allie was up to and if she was okay. Closing my eyes only seemed to make the flurry of those thoughts intensify. So I kept them open.

After a while, they adjusted to the darkness. Like a camera coming into focus, I was able to discern the myriad of dark shapes in the room, including his.

I watched as Dave crept about the room. He grabbed his clothes from the dresser, slowly pulling each drawer open. To ensure he remained quiet, he didn't close his sock drawer —it squeaks.

After pulling on pants and a shirt, he made for the door. He twisted the knob fully before silently prying it open.

"Where are you going?" My voice was hoarse.

He didn't say anything. He just stood there, dumbstruck.

I cleared my throat. "I guess this means you want to leave me here?"

"Constance," he whispered. "It's not that I don't want you to go."

"Then what is it, Dave?"

"It's, uh." He looked away, down the hallway. "What about the girls?"

"Mom's here. She'll look after them."

"Right." His sigh told me everything. He searched for another excuse.

"You might need me," I said. "You might need magic."

He sighed again. "I doubt it."

"So, you don't want me to go?"

"It's not that. I just think it's better if I go alone."

He thinks it's better.

That made one of us.

"Whatever it is," I said. "I'll understand. But you have to talk to me. Why can't I go?"

"It's complicated."

"So was healing you last night, but I did it anyway."

Dave let out a conceding grunt. "I guess we'll talk about it in the car."

I threw off the covers, slipped out of bed, and changed with speed, not silence. Yanking my drawers open, I grabbed my camping jeans, a pair of woolly socks, and a thermal top. No matter how unseasonably warm it was in Creel Creek, the mountain played by its own rules.

Dave made a pot of coffee. He stood near the kitchen window, peering outside at the dark sky above. The moon had disappeared.

"We're going to stop by the station real quick," Dave said. "There's an ATV on a trailer in the yard. It'll take five minutes to hitch one up. Better to be prepared in case she veered away from the camp. Tracking her down on foot could take all day."

"And how do you plan on tracking her down?" I grabbed a couple of Thermoses from the cabinet.

"I've still got my nose." His kind eyes found mine, and for the first time that morning, he broke into a smile. But it was short-lived.

"What is it?"

He held his nose next to the coffee maker and sniffed. "No. No. Not this. You can't be serious. That stupid, *stupid* potion." He shook his head. "My sense of smell—it's gone."

I smiled back at him. "Good thing you're bringing me."

The *I told you so* was implied.

We drove out of Creel Creek in a focused silence. Me trying to read Dave's thoughts—I couldn't—and Dave's eyes squinting through the morning layer of fog that clung to the town each morning no matter what the weatherman called for.

Finally, I couldn't take it anymore. "Are you ever going to tell me what you're *really* worried about?"

"It's nothing, really."

"It's something."

"It *is* something," he agreed. "I'm just not sure you'll understand."

"Seriously?" I wanted to laugh, but the mood in the car was too serious. "I thought we were past the whole you're not going to understand thing. For Gaia's sake, I'm a witch. I deal with magic every day."

"Constance, I know you're a witch, and you're engaged to a werewolf. So, this shouldn't be so hard for me to explain. But it is."

I knew he said other words, but my mind was still stuck on one.

"Engaged?" I eyed my rather empty ring finger.

"That's not what I meant to say," he said. "I meant you're with a werewolf. We've been together a while now."

"And we're not engaged." The words slipped out of my mouth with venom. Although I wasn't sure why. The topic had been skirted around for over a year—basically since I'd moved in with him.

When it did come up—usually when one of the girls saw something about marriage on TV—one of us snuffed it out. I assumed he wasn't ready. I wasn't sure I was either.

Flustered, Dave pinched the bridge of his nose. "Do you want to know what I've been worried about or what?"

I nodded. But my curiosity wasn't as piqued as it'd been that morning watching him try to sneak out. Something else was building up inside me, twisting my stomach into knots and threatening to turn my blood to lava.

I averted my gaze out the window, trying to ignore the throbbing in my chest. Had Dave just said he didn't want to marry me, or was I reading way too much into those words?

"It's the curse," he said. "I'm afraid Allie won't exactly be herself when we find her this morning."

"Okay?" I shrugged. "I'm sure the first change is the hardest."

"It's not *just* that. This is what I've been trying to talk to her about. But no matter how many times I've tried to artic-ulate it—it's just too hard to grasp it until it actually happens."

I swallowed hard and tried to focus on what he was saying.

"See, when it happens—when I shift... something else—someone else—takes over. And while he's only supposed to be let out with the moon, well, let's just say he does his best to stick around a while."

"So, you mean Allie won't be herself because she's not? She's this *other* thing?"

He nodded slowly. "It took me ages to control my guy— to keep him locked up until the very moment the moon rises, then bury him deep down when it sets. She'll get there, but today, I'm going to have to help Allie coax the other her back to where she belongs."

"Maybe I can help with that too," I offered.

"Maybe you can." He stared at the road. "And I'm sorry about before. I won't let it happen again."

With those words, my whole body went numb. Tears stung the corners of my eyes. I brushed them away, hoping without hope Dave hadn't noticed.

In the rearview mirror, his eyes betrayed him. They darted away from my gaze just as fast as his heart was running away from mine.

7

IN WITCH WE FIND A BODY IN THE WOODS

A strange stillness hung in the air along with smatterings of thick fog. Most had cleared away with the sun, but there were still patches on the ground. Another layer extended even higher, up to the tree-tops, most of which were barren of any leaves.

Despite Dave's promise of it being faster, the ATV seemed to inch through the dense forest with agonizing slowness. *How much longer will we have to search?*

We climbed higher up the mountain. Every now and then, I'd spot what had once been a pile of snow but was now a melted pool on the ground.

We drove on, Dave carefully navigating around brush and mud until we came across a game path. He stopped the ATV, and I cast a spell to find Allie.

My heart raced faster with each passing second. I didn't know why, except something felt off.

Someone.

Dave's whole demeanor was strange. He wasn't nearly as confident of finding her as he'd been earlier that morning.

"This way." I pointed down the path.

"The same direction," Dave said. "That's a good sign. I think I recognize these woods."

They all looked the same to me. Tree after tree after Mother-Gaia-forsaken tree.

We bounced along for another half-mile or so, the spell continuing to point my fingertip southwesterly.

"Allie!" Dave called. "Allie-girl! Allie-cat!"

Nothing.

We continued on through the brush.

"Allie?"

"I'm over here," a small voice sounded in the distance.

Dave jumped off the still moving ATV, and it shuddered to a stop beneath me, engine stalling.

I knew where I stood in the order of importance.

"Allie-cat, where are you?" Dave ran ahead.

I jogged behind him.

"Down here."

Dave lunged over fallen branches, skidded over rocks, then sprinted the distance between us and the sound of Allie's voice.

The teenager was sitting atop the trunk of a fallen hemlock tree. She'd found a blue tarp and wrapped it around herself.

Allie was rocking back and forth there, anxious even after spotting us coming down the mountainside.

"Are you okay?" Dave asked her. "Is she gone?"

"Is who gone?"

"Never mind." Dave shook his head. "You're okay. That's all that matters."

"Yeah, sure, Dad, I'm fine," Allie said, a touch of sarcasm dripping from her voice. "But I don't think he is."

Dave's brow furrowed, as if he didn't understand the joke.

I didn't either.

Then my eyes followed her gaze, down to a decrepit hunting blind.

Perched precariously about two feet above the ground, it was nothing more than a small hutch with a single doorway and narrow slits carved into three of its walls. The exterior slats were decayed and frail.

Beneath it was nothing more than mud and a large pile of leaves.

But that wasn't true. What my eyes had mistaken for leaves came into focus. It was a body. A man.

It looked as if he'd stepped out from the open entryway and fell flat on his face, never to get up again. His features were buried in the mud. His clothes were tattered and torn. There was a smattering of leaves built around him.

My stomach did a somersault.

Not again.

Just how many dead bodies was I destined to come across? Surely, I'd reached my quota.

Dave crept closer to the body. He eyed it warily, as if it might move.

As we came up to it, I understood his trepidation. The clothes weren't just torn; they were slashed. Most prominent amongst the tears were four large gashes across the back of the shirt, revealing a back that had more akin with hamburger meat than human flesh.

My heart sank.

Somewhere—anywhere else—these gashes might be mistaken for a bear or maybe a mountain lion.

Not here in Creel Creek. Not the morning after a full moon.

There was only one thing that could've made gashes like that. One person. And she was staring back at us with teary eyes and a trembling lip.

8

CONSTANCE CAMPBELL AND
ANOTHER DEAD BODY

D ave lingered between Allie and the body, doing his best to shield her from the gruesome sight.

Except he didn't have to. Perched atop the log, Allie stared down at her bare feet, the soles of which were covered in dirt. The tops had taken on a purplish hue from the cold.

I wondered how long Allie had been here before we got to her. Had she discovered the body and waited? Had she found it upon waking? Or was this all happening in real time?

For her sake, I hoped the latter.

"Your clothes." I went to hand her a bag filled with her undergarments, jeans, a sweater, and tennis shoes. She disregarded it.

"Da-da-da-dad," she stammered. "Is he... is he dead?"

Dave went to speak but the words didn't come.

I'd never seen it take so long for Dave to go into work mode. Crimefighting Dave was the man I'd fallen in love with.

This man was something else. Someone else.

A scared father.

"What can I do?" I asked.

"I don't know." Dave squeezed his eyes shut, pushing his palms against them. He exhaled slowly, trying desperately to shake away from this nightmare.

But the nightmare wasn't going away.

The longer he stayed silent, the more scared, the more isolated, I felt. There was no telling the toll it was taking on Allie. The girl began to shake with chills. Finally, she took the clothes and changed under the tarp.

We couldn't just stand around in the cold waiting for an answer that would never come. Someone had to do something. I just couldn't believe that someone was me.

"Maybe we should call this in?" I suggested, finally.

"Maybe." His hands fell to his sides, and Dave stared at me for a long moment. Then he smiled. It was meant to be reassuring, but it conveyed the opposite. It was bittersweet and sad. "I should probably take a look around first."

There he is.

Dave scrubbed his face, then he began to scour the ground beside the body. He nodded and grunted several times before trotting around the exterior of the hunting blind.

His boots crunched over fallen leaves. They were the only part of him visible when his voice sounded from the other side.

"Allie," he said softly, as if not to startle her. "Do you remember anything about last night?"

"Not really." She sounded like any other teenager, unconvincing and unsure.

"Nothing?"

"Just flashes," she said. "Nothing concrete."

Dave nodded, as if he were expecting this. "Where did

you wake up this morning? Were you down here beside him?"

She shook her head. "Farther up the mountain. Maybe half a mile."

"What'd I tell you about waking up?"

"To stay put." Except for quick glances, she continued to gaze anywhere other than the body. Eventually, she buried her face in her hands.

"Why didn't you?" Dave asked. "I mean why didn't you stay put?"

"Because I was cold. And you said we'd wake up together."

"I think you know why I wasn't there."

"The potion." Allie lifted her chin, her fingers webbed around her eyes. "Dad, I wasn't going to take it. I promise. I didn't mean for you to either—"

"I know you didn't mean for any of this." Dave came around the other side of the shack. He took one look at those sad eyes and froze. "Let's not worry about any of that. Not now anyway. Tell me, what do you remember from last night? This morning? Did you talk to the *other* you?"

"What do you mean the *other* me?" she asked.

"So, that's a no." Dave poked his head inside the entryway. "I'm guessing that tarp came from inside there?"

"No." Allie pointed to a mound of loose soil. "It was over there, covering the clay."

"Interesting." Dave leveled his gaze on Allie and asked the question on everyone's mind. "Honey, do you think you did this?"

Allie refused to answer.

"Well?" Dave's dark eyes softened. "Do you? Be honest."

"I, uh, I'm not sure. Dad, I... I remember chasing someone. That's all."

"You remember chasing me. There's nothing here suggesting this man was running anywhere."

"Still. This looks pretty bad."

"Looks can be deceiving," Dave said.

"What do you mean?" I asked.

"Just a feeling. Like it almost looks staged."

"Oh?"

I hadn't been thinking in those terms. But Dave was right. There was nothing indicating this man was using the hunting blind. There was no gun. No pack of supplies. No food. It was like he was just here, in the wrong place at the wrong time.

Or maybe the right place at the right time, if you wanted to suggest he was attacked by a werewolf.

"Something else is odd about this place," Dave said. "I got a big hit of deja vu as soon as we walked down. I feel like I've been in this very spot before. Like something else happened right here. Except I can't remember what."

"Maybe you were in wolf form?"

"Maybe." He nodded, then squinted, as if he was struck with a thought.

"You remember?"

"No." He shook his head. "But while you're here, do you mind performing a summoning spell? Something that might find any magical clues in the area?"

Thinking it might come to this, I'd been trying to gather some of my strength back. After spending so much magical energy the previous night with him and in the search for Allie that morning, my reserves were depleted.

Regardless, I worked a spell.

"Magical feeling. Magic revealing.
With this scene in view. Help us to find a clue.

Whether it be a thought, a word, or sound.
If there's something hidden, let it be found."

We waited and nothing happened. Not a gust of wind. Not the chirp of a bird. No sound or whisper. Nothing at all.

"Maybe that's a good thing?" Dave shrugged.

"Why is that good?" Allie's brow furrowed.

"Well," Dave said. "It could mean there was no magic involved in this death. No magic, no werewolf."

"But it also might mean my magic is spent." I hated to be the bearer of bad news when they'd both perked up a bit.

"Then prove it." Dave's rapt attention was on me now.

"How am I supposed to do that?"

"I don't know." He threw up his hands. "Perform another spell. If it doesn't work, then your magic is spent. But if it does, then maybe there was no magic involved here."

He gave me a pleading look. This wasn't for him. It was for Allie—she needed the reassurance.

I just wasn't sure I could give her any.

I searched for inspiration but didn't find any. I could make the wind blow, but then I'd never be quite sure if it was really my spell. I could make a tree fall, knowing it would make a sound, but it might also disturb the scene.

Finally, I decided on something simple. I readied the spell, whispered it into the air, and prayed for it to work.

The dirt rose a few feet off the ground, maneuvered like a helicopter to a spot a few feet away, then dropped suddenly with a splash of loose soil.

It was perfect in execution and perfect as proof that my magic wasn't spent.

If only it hadn't revealed another body.

———

COMPARED TO THE OTHER BODY, these remains were far from fresh. It was an orderly set of bones, as intact as the skeleton of a college anatomy classroom.

Dave's stare went vacant, staring past me at the skeleton nearly twenty feet away. He shook his head slightly.

"What is it?" I asked.

"Nothing," he said. "We'll talk about it later."

"Then it's not nothing."

"I don't know what it is," he said flatly.

Aside from Allie's presence, I didn't see a reason we couldn't talk about it now. Whatever *it* was. But I didn't press.

"What's the plan?" Allie asked. "Are we staying out here all day?"

"No." Dave's eyes kept pinging from one dead body to the next. "We'll go back to the car, Constance will take you home, and I'll call Mac."

I either failed to comprehend the order of operations or Dave wasn't making sense. "So, we'll leave before he gets here?"

"That's right."

I narrowed my eyes. "Won't that look a little strange?"

Dave swallowed hard. It took him a long beat to respond. "Listen. No one saw me get the ATV this morning. I'll say you dropped me off out here with it last night."

"Okay... why though?"

"Because"—he glanced at Allie—"no one has to know she was out here last night. Not Mac. Not anyone."

"But Dad—" Allie began to protest.

Dave stifled her with a finger. "You didn't do this, sweetheart. Actually, let me put it another way. A werewolf didn't kill that man. Someone staged it to look like one did. And this—this other body—you definitely didn't do that."

By the tone of his voice, it seemed almost as if Dave knew who did.

"You're sure you don't want us to stay?" I asked him.

"Positive," he said. "There's no reason for her to get wrapped up in this. No reason for you to either."

"But Dad—"

"Allie, don't. As far as this town is concerned, I'm the *only* werewolf in Creel Creek. For now, we should keep it that way. There's enough prejudice as it is. And trust me, a case like this will bring out a lot of it."

Allie shrugged. "Still doesn't feel right."

Because it's not, I thought.

Dave was gifted at explaining away paranormal crimes to the normal citizens of Creel Creek. A hunter breaking in and killing a shifter with a sword might become a domestic dispute between rival factions.

There was a kernel of truth in there.

But this? This didn't sit right.

"What about me?" I asked.

"You've done enough already. You proved there's no magic involved. I think that's enough for now. Don't you?"

No.

"I guess."

I hated when we had this type of interaction. Dave usually wanted, or often needed, my help. That was until he didn't.

At a certain point, the dividing line between cop and civilian always reared its ugly head.

This moment felt a tad premature.

I could see into the future. Not really—I don't have that power—but I could already tell I was going to be more involved than Dave wanted me to be.

I was like a young—younger—Jessica Fletcher, having to

skirt around law enforcement instead of working alongside them. It was much more understandable on *Murder, She Wrote*—I don't believe Jessica ever shared a bed with Sheriff Tupper.

"Constance," he said placatingly. "I can't be in two places at once. I need your help with—with her," he whispered, as if he didn't know Allie's hearing was as fine-tuned as his own.

Allie let out a huge sigh. "I'm not a baby, Dad. Stop treating me like one. We can stay here. It's not a big deal."

"It is a big deal," Dave argued. "Mac is thorough. He won't jump to conclusions. Not with me. But his prejudice against our kind is deep. If he were to see you out here, know that you changed, know that it was the first time and you were alone last night... well, I don't think I could stop him from doing some poor man's algebra. Trust me. It's better if I'm here alone."

Most members of the sheriff's department were sympathetic to Dave's abnormality. Almost all of his deputies were shifters of various varieties. They'd even allowed Dave into their fraternity—the League of Artemis, giving him a talisman so he could shift into wolf form without the full moon while keeping his mind intact.

Regardless, they still viewed him as somewhat of an outsider.

Mac, a fox shifter and Dave's lead detective, was chief skeptic.

"Then why call Mac?"

"Because Mac will be discrete. This is our jurisdiction. It would look off for me to call anyone else. We'll have to get help identifying the body—bodies. But otherwise, we can keep this in house."

"Don't you have another detective?"

"It's not like I can take the lead. Like I said, it will look odd enough as it is. This situation is, uh, unique."

"What if Mac thinks you staged the body? And how exactly do you plan to explain both?"

"He won't think that. He trusts me. And I don't know. Wolves dig like any other canine. I'll tell him I smelled it and dug it up."

"So that's your plan then? To lie. To use Mac's trust. Dress things up like you were out here last night—like you stumbled across this body—bodies?"

It wasn't in Dave's nature to cover up a crime—a characteristic most would desire in their sheriff. While I'd seen him set aside the paranormal clues for the benefit of normal law enforcement, I'd never seen him completely omit facts, especially not to his own department.

Lying to Mac was the beginning of a slippery slope—a slope I didn't think Dave could navigate down without help.

This reeked of bad decision making. I was going to let him know it.

"What happens if—when—Mac finds out about Allie? What happens if he finds out about you? About what happened last night? About the ATV this morning? Dave, what happens when he finds out you lied to him? Multiple lies? Do you really want to go to jail? To put the girls through that?"

"I haven't lied to him... yet."

"But that's your plan..."

"It is my plan. And it's going to stay my plan unless either of you come up with something better."

"I've got nothing." Allie turned her anxious eyes on me.

"I think the truth will set you free," I said.

Dave shook his head wearily.

"I know how Mac can be," I said. "But it's like you said—this place was staged. If we just show him—"

"He'll blame you," Dave said. "He'll say you used your magic to manipulate the scene."

I hated to admit it, but Dave was right. How many times had Mac and I butted heads? How many times had I prevented him from convicting the wrong man?

Too many.

Maybe it was better to leave Allie out of it.

I sighed. "I guess I don't have a better idea."

"Think!" Dave rubbed his own temples. "There has to be some other solution."

I knew he was talking to himself, but Allie didn't comprehend as much.

"Couldn't we just leave them here?" She shrugged. "Someone else is bound to find them. One day. It doesn't have to be us."

"Allie," I said kindly. "That's someone's loved one. What would you do if someone you loved went missing? Who knows how long the body that was buried has been there with their family praying they might turn up somewhere."

Dave began to say something, then he stiffened. His voice took on a gravely tone. "Leave the past in the past. We can bury both bodies."

"What?" I asked, confused.

Allie noticed it too. She squinted up at her father. "Dad, are you all right?"

"I'm fine," he growled. He shuddered, as if snapping out of a trance. "We're not going to bury the bodies. Not again."

"Good," I said. "Because *we* never suggested it. Dave, are you sure you're all right?"

He let out a slow sigh. "Sorry, but this is a stressful situation. I should never have lashed out like that. I just want—I need—you two to listen to me for a change. I've made up my mind. You're leaving. I'm staying. I'm calling Mac, and I'm telling him I was out here alone."

"Dave—"

"Don't." He grimaced. "No matter what you say from here to the car, that's it—I'm not changing my mind."

9

CREEL CREEK AFTER DARK
SEASON 3: EPISODE 12

It's getting late.
So very late.
You hear something go bump in the night.
Are you afraid?
You should be!
Welcome to Creel Creek After Dark.

Athena: Good evening, folks. I'm your host, Athena Hunter. With me today is my cohost, Ivana Steak, and this, well, this is *Creel Creek After Dark*.

Ivana: That's right, Athena. For reasons we'd rather not get into, it's been quite a while since our audience last heard from us. Some of you have been waiting patiently and some kindly—we appreciate every email those of you sent.

Athena: What about the others?

Ivana: You mean those *other* emails? The phone calls. The midnight doorbell ring. By the way, I know that was you, Bobo! I have a security camera and as of last week, a restraining order.

Athena: What Ivana is trying to say is we appreciate the sentiment, but we'd ask you to refrain from such tactics in the future.

Ivana: Or else.

Athena: Or else what, Ivana?

Ivana: I can't say words like that on the air—at least not in most states. For now, let's keep to our usual doses of witty banter and playful puns. Speaking of, maybe it's time we refresh our audience, the old and the new, with what exactly we do here on *Creel Creek After Dark.*

Athena: Well, we're a weekly—when it's convenient—Podcast and ParaTube Show with guests, stories, and announcements from Virginia's most paranormal town, Creel Creek.

Ivana: And while not everything that comes out of our mouths has been verified as absolute truth, none of it has been disproven either. In fact, I'd go so far as to say our position has only been solidified over these past few years.

Athena: What I think Ivana is trying to say is while sometimes we speculate, we never fabricate. First and foremost, we hope to entertain.

Ivana: Don't be putting words in my mouth, Athena. What I was trying to say—before I was so rudely interrupted—is on several occasions now, we've bore witness to the paranormal. We've seen people do amazing things. We witnessed a thousand birds attack a conference stage. And don't forget, I was—

Athena: Going off script?

Ivana: We don't have scripts. We have outlines.

Athena: True. And today's outline—no matter how much you wish otherwise—has nothing to do with you.

Ivana: Fair point, Athena. Although, it's funny because I thought you wanted a change of topic.

Athena: I didn't necessarily say that.

Ivana: You didn't have to say anything. I can see it in your notes. I can see it in your beautiful brown eyes right now. Your heart isn't in this one. You, like so many others around Creel Creek, want to cover for him. And we're done with that.

Athena: Ivana—

Ivana: Don't Ivana me. What I'm trying to get to, what brought us back together in the first place—what seems to always bring us together—was a murder. Our local authority figures wish for us to believe it was simply an animal attack—a bear, if can you believe. In the height of hibernation? I think not.

Athena: Ivana—

Ivana: In my eyes, there's only one suspect. A man who bites his own tail at every press conference. A man who covers up twice the paranormal activity that we uncover. And if I'm not mistaken, it's a man who howls at every full moon. You know who I'm talking about.

10

DAVE MARSTERS AND THE
COVER-UP

Despite my feeble protests, Dave didn't change his mind.

We left him at the campsite, stranded with his phone, a radio, and the ATV beside its trailer.

I watched him in the rearview mirror, hoping he might put up his hands to stop us. Hoping he might change his mind.

Allie slumped into her usual spot in the passenger seat of Dave's Interceptor while I had trouble adjusting the driver's seat to my liking. I'd never driven it before. Despite the differences between a regular SUV and the police version being negligible, the car felt foreign under my control.

I couldn't find anything I wanted—like a good radio station or the windshield wiper spray setting when bird poop splattered into my purview. Worse than that, it felt as if I was always on the cusp of turning on the overhead lights. I knew exactly where the switch was to turn them on. Still, I kept checking it was in the off position every few minutes.

We took the long way home, nearly two hours out of the

way, through Charlottesville and around to the opposite end of Creel Creek.

It didn't matter how tinted the windows were, I was sure every car we passed could see inside the vehicle. They could spot us as frauds parading around in a police car. Somehow, they also knew we were aiding and abetting criminal behavior.

Because that's what it was—Dave's lie had criminal repercussions. His fabricated story was equally as bad as the scene we'd found.

I counted out the lies in my head.

One. He hadn't wolfed out the night of the full moon.

Two. He didn't come across the body alone.

And three. He definitely hadn't dug up the *other* body.

I tried to tell myself these were decent lies. We'd catch the true culprit in the end.

It didn't matter to my stomach, which continued to churn with a sour mix of emotions.

When we got to the house, Allie locked herself in her room. I couldn't blame her. She'd had a long night and an even worse morning. Plus, her sisters were up and at 'em in every way possible. They were loud, practically bouncing off the walls, and they wanted to know everything about Allie's first night as a wolf.

"Let her sleep, girls," I told them.

I didn't know if Allie would sleep or if she'd just console herself with music and other distractions.

Either way, I hoped she wasn't letting her stray thoughts fester. I was doing enough of that for the both of us.

I recapped everything for Mom and for Brad, then I made dinner and got the girls to bed before Dave finally dragged himself through the door.

Mac dropped him off.

In the few hours we'd been apart, time had done a number on him. He had dark blue bags under his eyes, and his stubble had grown into a five o'clock the next day shadow. His uniform was wrinkled, his shirt untucked on the side and back.

Dave, the consummate professional, was a thing of the past.

"How'd it go?" I grabbed his plate from the microwave.

"Spaghetti?" He smiled wearily. "You spoil me."

I rolled my eyes. "Sorry, I didn't make a gourmet meal."

"I didn't mean it like that. I'm sorry. I really do appreciate everything you do here. I know I don't deserve it. Especially not today."

"You're stalling," I said. "What happened?"

"Nothing happened. Everything happened. Police work happened."

"What about Mac? He believed you?"

"He had no reason not to."

Except that it was all a lie.

I stared at Dave, unflinching as he twirled noodles onto his fork and took a bite.

"You really want a play-by-play?"

"Kinda." I didn't tell him how much of the day I'd spent afraid he was going to get arrested and afraid a deputy might show up at the door for Allie.

"Well, let me put it this way. Mac wanted to stop by Mac-Donald's on the way home. Get it?" He laughed at his own dad joke. "When I told him I'd rather eat a shoe, he made a dog joke."

"So, if he's making jokes, he must not suspect you're involved?"

"I don't think so. And the medical examiner came out to look. We talked it over a bit. The tears on the flesh—they were artificially made. Done with some sort of tool to make it look as if he was attacked by an animal. But the marks weren't made by claws. He said he's never seen anything quite like it."

"Does he have any idea who the man is?"

"We're waiting on IDs for both bodies. One's going to take longer than the other."

Both bodies.

His words struck a nerve.

"Are you going to tell me about the other body?"

"What do you mean? You were there. You saw it."

"You're right. I saw it. And I saw you. There's something you're not telling me."

"Like what?"

I shrugged. "I don't know. Something. I saw it in your eyes."

He shook his head. "Let me finish eating. We'll continue this upstairs."

I didn't think it mattered where we talked. But Mom was in the living room watching TV. Whatever this was, Dave didn't want her to hear it.

He didn't seem so eager for me to either. Upstairs, he went straight for the shower. It ran for a long time, billowing steam from the cracked doorway.

I waited impatiently, not daring to open the paperback I had beside my bed.

I guiltily shooed Mom away when she knocked on the bedroom door. Our nightly story could wait for tomorrow.

Tonight, Dave's story was all that mattered.

A MYRIAD OF troubling thoughts began to find their way into my head.

What if Dave had killed someone?

I remembered what he'd said about his other self— about the state we might find Allie in.

I knew werewolves were controlled by their curse. They didn't have full control of what they did—and who they hurt —when in shifted form.

They didn't have memories from it either.

Dave told me once about waking up next to a deer carcass, his lips and hands covered in blood, but no memory of killing the deer. That was enough for me to never ask about his nights again.

Had Dave been struck by a similar memory?

No, that's silly. Dave would never. He could never do something like that.

He slipped out of the bathroom in boxer shorts, his chest glistening. His hair was stringy and damp. Stray beads of water freckled across his collar bone.

He brushed a towel against his chest, staring at me with an expression on his face I couldn't quite read.

I waited.

He gathered himself, swallowing hard. "I'd prefer *not* to tell you. I mean if that's okay?"

"Dave," I said. "We've always told each other the truth. Or at least I have. Even when it's hard. And trust me, it's been hard."

"There's a difference between hard and... and this." He massaged his temples. "Besides, I've got this *killer* headache."

The word killer shot bile into my throat.

"A headache? Really? That's your excuse? I guess you won't be doing anything strenuous tonight anyway."

He chuckled. "Constance, I'm serious. I think it's best for us not to have this conversation. Probably ever."

"Best for who?"

"For me, obviously. I don't want this to change us, but I'm afraid—no, I'm sure it will."

"Then I think we have to talk this out," I said.

"We don't." Dave pinched the bridge of his nose. "That body doesn't change the man I am today. The man you fell in love with. It's in the past. It's something that never needed to be uncovered."

My heart was sinking fast. I wasn't being silly before. He *had* killed someone. I was sure I was right.

"But it was uncovered," I argued. "Isn't it best if you tell me now? Whatever this is, we can work through it. But I have to know. What happens when Mac or whoever else finds out?

Dave shook his head. "They won't find anything worthwhile. I promise you that."

"You're making a lot of promises lately. And telling a lot of lies. Let me be honest with you, Dave. Those bodies—both of them—already changed the way I look at you. Today was, well, it was the worst day I've had since my father died. Whatever you say right now, it can only help your case."

"It won't." Dave's hands returned to his temples. "And my head really is pounding."

"I'd tell you to go get some ibuprofen from the bathroom, but it might take you another eternity to come back. I'll get you some."

I sprang from the bed to get Dave medicine.

By the time I returned, he was in bed with the covers pulled up to his chest. His eyes were closed.

I put the pills on his nightstand with a tall glass of water.

"Not allowed," I said. "You're not going to sleep until I get some sort of explanation."

"You're sure?" An eye blinked opened while the other stayed squeezed shut. "Cause if I tell you, it can't be taken back."

"You make it sound like you murdered this man." There. I said it. "Dave, you didn't murder him. Did you?"

"No." His voice was a whisper.

I exhaled the breath I'd been holding. That was something at least. But it didn't explain what he knew. "So, what is it then? What happened out there today?"

"A memory." His hand fumbled on the nightstand for the pills, nearly knocking the glass over.

"What kind of memory?" This felt like pulling teeth.

Dave popped the pills in his mouth and swallowed. "A memory from other me."

I struggled to understand where this was going. "Do you mean you know who did?"

"My father," he said. "Seems like I helped him bury the body the next day."

"That was the memory?"

Dave made a singular nod into his chest.

"How old were you?"

"Fourteen or so." Dave closed both eyes again. "I can barely remember anything. The other me was still in control at the time."

"Then it's not your fault. Right?"

"Not my fault." He laughed gruffly. "Then whose fault is it?"

"Your father's?"

I choked back the bile building in my throat, and a sob burst out. My eyes flooded with tears.

How was I supposed to react to truth like this?

Dave hadn't betrayed me. This was nothing like what happened with my lying ex.

He hadn't lied. Not really. His *other* self had.

Even then, he was just a kid. A teen wolf, so to speak.

Like Allie.

I'd already seen what kind of havoc the combination could have. Allie created the daylight potion to try to get out of situations just like this.

My heart hurt for Dave's teenage self, helping his father dig a hole in the woods. But it hurt even more for the man beside me. He was equally scared, clawing for solutions to problems he should never have had to answer to begin with.

"What are you thinking, Constance?" Dave struggled to lift his eyes open. When they did, they were pleading.

"I think it's a lot to take in."

"It *is* that." Dave blinked, his eyes staying shut a long second before popping back open. "I hope you understand why I got so... so confused earlier."

"I got it," I said. "Or rather, I get it. But what happens now? What if that body *is* linked to your father? I know he's been dead a long time, but still, it'd look bad for you, wouldn't it?"

Dave's pleading eyes squinted with new emotion.

Desperation, maybe?

"Constance," he said in a whisper. "I never told you my father was dead."

11

A FORGOTTEN FATHER

Dave's eyes drooped closed.

"What?" I nearly screamed.

Nothing. Dave's eyes stayed closed.

"Dave!" I grabbed him by the shoulder.

He made a loud snore, then his breathing shallowed again without waking.

I thought long and hard about slapping him, but then I thought better.

Between his night without the change, his long day of work, and now this headache, there wasn't enough left in the tank.

Either that or he was good at faking.

With a deep breath, I thought long and hard about what he'd just said. He never told me his father was dead.

Does that mean what I think?

It had to.

But what had led me to believe that *both* his parents were dead?

I knew Dave's mother had died during his senior year of

high school. A congenital heart defect had gone undetected until ultimately she had a heart attack.

We'd talked a lot about how hard that year had been on him and his family. The milestones—the dances, the last football game, and the graduation walk—were all done without her there.

My own senior year had been similar. But I had my father to lean on then.

Dave didn't. He told me his father had withdrawn himself from Dave's life around this time, leaving Dave and Imogene alone to fend for themselves. His father spent long nights at the bar dealing with his grief.

Dave always used the past tense when talking about his father. I'd just assumed his father drank himself to death, as so many do.

So, was I in the wrong for not explicitly asking?

Or were Dave's omissions to blame?

Omissions are lies.

To think, Dave's father was out there somewhere in the world. I wondered how long they'd been out of touch. At least as long as I'd known Dave but probably longer.

Did he know Dave's wife died? That he was a grandfather? He sure as hell didn't know about me.

And what about Imogene? Had she lost touch with him too?

If Dave wasn't going to be awake enough for my questions, at least the change in time zones meant Imogene was.

In fact, she was probably setting the dinner table now. I typed a text and guiltily hit send.

ME: Hey, Im, do you have a minute?

IMOGENE: Not really. Just got home from soccer practice. About to start supper. Why? What's up?

ME: Do you ever speak to your dad?

THREE DOTS CAME AND WENT. Then they came and went again. And again. Finally, her message came through.

IMOGENE: I haven't spoken to him in over twenty years. As far as I know, neither has Dave. Why? Did he contact you?!?

ME: No.

IMOGENE: Did he contact Dave?!?!

ME: No.

IMOGENE: Then what's up???

IMOGENE: ???

ME: It's, uh, it's complicated, but I'm just finding out your father is even alive. I thought otherwise.

IMOGENE: Oh...

IMOGENE: What do you mean by complicated?

ME: Dave kind of passed out before he could tell me anything.

IMOGENE: He passed out?!? What happened last night? Oh crap! I forgot to FaceTime Allie this morning. Is she okay? Did other her stick around a while?

ME: Also complicated. But other her is gone. Call me before you call her.

IMOGENE: Will do. Give me like ten...

IN THE STILL SILENCE OF the dark room, I waited for Imogene's call. I lay there wondering how things could get so complicated so fast. I longed for the days of old when every day was the same. Monotonous, yes. But at least I didn't have a crisis to deal with every few months.

"Life is one long crisis." Brad's voice boomed in my head, startling me and making me jump to my feet.

Except my feet weren't ready. I dropped face first on the carpet—a lot like the body in the woods.

Brad!

"What? It's not like your brain has a ringer? If it did, you'd still be jumpy when it rang."

Fair enough. But to my point, it's only been a few years since I became a witch. And over those years, it seems like I've been jumping from one crisis to the next.

"Oh, and your life was so perfect before? No complications? Your mother didn't disappear when you were young?

To be fair, that's kind of related to these others.

"Excuse me. Let me think of another. You didn't marry a man in Vegas only to annul it a few weeks later?"

We weren't technically married. And you can stop. I get it. Life is complicated.

"As it turns out, so is eternal life."

Oh? Is there something you need to get off your chest?

"Not tonight," Brad said. *"Tonight, I wanted to check in with you. It's been a long day."*

And getting even longer, I thought. *Dave lied to me about his father. Sort of. I think he lied. And, get this. His father is the one who killed that guy.*

"Which guy?"

The skeleton. Inwardly, I eye rolled.

Brad took no time with his response. *"I've heard of skeletons in the closet, but they aren't usually so real. You know, this is why people warned you not to date a werewolf."*

Dave didn't do it though. His father did.

"But he could, Constance. He could kill. All it takes is one bad night."

Meaning?

"Meaning werewolves can't control what they do at the full moon. They're monsters. And I mean that in the kindest and most delicate way possible. It doesn't matter how much Dave wants to be good. He can go twenty-seven days being a saint—the best version of himself. But the night he turns, all bets are off. If someone crosses his path, it won't end well... for them."

Got it, I thought, wishing there was a way for me to disconnect the call. *Slam.*

"Were you trying to hang up on me?" Brad asked.

That was the idea.

"Uh, okay then. I see how it is. If that's how it's going to be, then fine. I'll go hang out at your grandmother's house for a while."

Say hi to the cats for me.

"If you recall, spelling their litter box was my idea. I could've let you go on scooping it every few days."

Brad, I thought we were going to end this call?

"You were," he snapped. "I was trying to help you understand the quandary Dave's in. And you're right there with him."

What quandary?

"Someone tried to frame a werewolf."

Right. It's Creel Creek. Some people know there are werewolves.

"But they did so in the exact spot a werewolf killed before."

Oh. Brad couldn't hear my mind click, but it did.

"The chances of it being a coincidence are—"

Slim, I finished his thought.

"There. I said what I was here for. Bye now."

Not only had Brad driven his point home, he'd done so in such a way to jumpstart my already curious brain.

There was no way Mac was going to solve this case. Not without some help.

I didn't have much time to ponder. I wasn't off the metaphorical phone for long before my real phone lit up with a candid photo of Imogene and her two sons.

"Hey," I answered anxiously.

12

A FORGETFUL FATHER

Through Dave's background snores, I filled Imogene in on the happenings, from the full moon and Allie's potion making to Dave's not-so-cursed night. Finally, we got to the point about the bodies in the woods.

But I couldn't do it. I left out the details of their father's involvement. That was a can of worms I wasn't opening. Not over the phone, from thousands of miles away.

Dave could tell her on his own terms.

The rhythm of his breathing steadied slightly, and his body twisted to the side.

It was hard to stay mad at him, but I managed.

Imogene almost hung up before I could weasel anything from her about their father. Reluctantly, she gave me some shaky details.

She told me he left Creel Creek twenty years ago without so much as saying goodbye to either of his kids. He didn't tell them where he was going, nor did he leave a way to contact him. He didn't own a cell phone.

Basically, he disappeared. Except they'd both seen it

coming. She said from the time their mother passed, it felt inevitable.

I hung up the phone, and again I wasn't sure what to think. This barrage of new information stung, but I couldn't pinpoint why. Maybe because it wasn't Dave who told me about it.

Omissions are lies.

Dave let out another sigh, as if he could hear my thoughts.

Unable to even look in his direction, I rolled over to my side and formed a barrier between us with the blanket tucked beneath me.

But I woke a few hours later, expecting to find us closer. Our nightly pattern was to gravitate toward the other until Dave's arm found its way over my waist. But Dave hadn't moved, and I was too stubborn to inch my way over to his side.

I missed the graze of his breath on my shoulder. I missed the warmth of his feet, which usually radiated heat near my cold toes.

The bed was cold—colder than the wintery weather blowing into Creel Creek from West Virginia. And it stayed like that for the rest of the night.

I figured he was just too passed out to even care.

The next time I woke, I was sure of it. Dave was too passed out. His alarm, which usually chirped for a second before being silenced, continued to get louder and louder.

Dave wasn't moving to turn it off.

I watched the rise and fall of his chest, waiting for him to jerk away and slam his hand down on the clock.

Beep. Beep. Beep. It continued.

Finally, I jerked the covers off both of us, sprang out of bed, and slammed my fist down atop it, which kind of hurt and didn't actually stop its annoying chirp. I scrambled for the right button. When I found it, I let out a huzzah.

And Dave slept on.

His snores grated on my last nerve. I stomped around to my side, got back in bed, and stared straight at the ceiling for what felt like five minutes but was probably no more than thirty seconds.

I let out a long sigh.

Nothing.

No matter how many times I huffed or heaved, I couldn't will Dave to wake up.

That was until I did. I willed it with a light touch of magic and a few words.

"Sleep is for the dead, so let's get out of bed."

His eyes flashed open. He looked at me, startled, then shut his eyes tight again.

"What are you doing?" My words seemed to amplify the tension in the room.

"I *was* sleeping." His voice had a rasp to it, like he was gearing up to play the next Batman in Hollywood. "Why? What should I be doing?"

I pulled the blanket back to make space for me to sit up, then I stared. "Well, let's see. Normally, when your alarm goes off, you get up. And after a day like yesterday, you'd typically go into work."

"Work, huh?" His words came out like a growl. "And what if I don't feel like work?"

"I didn't think it was possible for you not to feel like work. You went in with the flu last month."

"Constance." He tripped over my name. "Anything is possible if you put your mind to it."

"Is that right?" I laughed derisively. "I can't believe you're trying to joke with me—after dropping a bombshell like you did last night."

"It wasn't a bombshell," he argued. "Not really. It was a misunderstanding."

"A misunderstanding? You could've told me a thousand times your father was still alive. You chose not to."

"What difference does it make if he's dead or gone? Either way, he's not here."

"I think you know there's a difference," I said.

"I haven't talked to the guy in twenty years. He's dead in every way that matters. Save one."

Twenty years was a long time to go without speaking to someone. By the look in Dave's eyes, it was clear he wouldn't mind going twenty more.

"And who knows," Dave continued. "There's a solid chance he's no longer with us. Then your whole argument is moot."

"It's not," I said, but the words came out defeated.

I hated this.

I hated to see Dave hurting. To see him struggle with the weight of what was squarely on his shoulders.

I couldn't even imagine what was going through his mind. His father had done something heinous, then he used him to cover up the crime.

Here I was mad because I thought he should have the decency to tell me straight-up if his father was dead or alive.

It wasn't fair. Not to either of us.

We couldn't change the past.

"Are you okay?" I asked.

"I think you know I'm not."

"Okay." I wasn't sure how to react to such brutal honesty from a man who kept so much close to his chest. "Anything I can do to help?"

His brow furrowed into a deep scowl. "I don't know. You could let me play dumb for a little while."

"You want to play dumb?"

"At least until I get my bearings. My head feels like it's been smashed by a sledgehammer." His eyes narrowed playfully. "You didn't hit me with a sledgehammer last night, did you?"

"I thought about it a time or two." I grinned. "But I'm not sure what you mean by play dumb. What does that entail?"

"Not much. But maybe you could give me a little grace today. I'm sorry I lied to you."

"I can do grace," I said. "Today only."

He yawned into a stretch. "What do you think I should be doing right now? Should I go into work?"

"Your head hurts that bad, huh?"

He nodded. "You have no idea."

"You think this is because of the other night?" I asked. "The potions—are they still in your system?"

"Something like that." He sat up and scratched the stubble on his chin in mock thought. "But hey, I'm supposed to be the dumb guy. I'll ask the questions."

I chuckled. I wasn't sure how to factor in the use of the daylight potion. But I remembered Gran telling us how it might affect the werewolf negatively. Dave's curse wasn't let out when it needed to be. Now, it was bottled up inside him.

"It's Sunday," I told him. "The girls are up. I can hear them."

"Huh," he grunted. "I guess that explains the squeaky sounds coming from down the hall."

I snorted this time. Even when I was mad at him, he could be funny.

"Maybe I did hit you on the head last night," I said.

"I knew it." He smiled.

Then he sprang from bed as if he were weightless. Still shirtless, he pulled on a pair of plaid pajama bottoms and made for the door. Before leaving the room entirely, he stretched at the door, his back muscles rippling.

"Not fair."

"What's not fair?" The harsh growl was back. But turning to look at me, his hardened features softened.

With his flash of anger, something woke inside of me. I didn't know what it was. But it was something. Something not good.

"Nothing," I said, allowing a thin smile to shape my lips.

"Good. Guess I'll see you down there." He strode down the hall, calling out, "Little ones. It's time to wake up."

I waited until his heavy footfalls were down the stairs before whispering to myself, "It isn't fair how much I'm still mad at you."

"WELCOME to the Bewitched House of Pancakes," Elsie greeted me in the kitchen.

"That's right. We serve pancakes twenty-four seven," Kacie added.

"Bewitched House of Pancakes." I laughed. "What makes them so bewitched?"

"Every fourth pancake is burnt," Kacie said.

Elsie nodded her agreement. "Twenty pancakes, every fourth pancake is burnt, and it's the seventh day of the week. Or is Sunday the first?"

"Depends on the calendar," I said.

Dave grunted.

"What's wrong?"

"You heard them. Look at all these burnt pancakes. It's like I've never done it before."

"These aren't good either." Elsie had a stack of unburned pancakes on her plate.

"They're fine if you have enough syrup."

"It looks like you took the whole bottle." Her plate was a pool of syrup with a single pancake drowning in the center.

"You." Dave narrowed his eyes. "What was your name again? Weren't you the one who told me the recipe?"

"Dad, you know I'm Kacie."

"Obviously I do. I was testing you more than anything. And I think you failed the test."

I nibbled the edge of a pancake. "Seems like you might've mixed up the baking soda with the baking powder."

"I mixed up?" Dave was incredulous. "She's to blame. That one over there."

"Dad!" Elsie moaned.

"I'm testing you again."

"That's Elsie." Kacie laughed.

"Right. Right. Elsie gave me the baking soda."

"I got mixed up," she said.

"Yeah, well, what am I supposed to do? I'm just a line cook."

"I'm head chef," Kacie said proudly.

"And whose idea was that?" I asked.

They pointed at Dave who shrugged nonchalantly. Even though I was mad at him, it was hard to find fault with his parenting techniques.

He was always a great dad—probably making up for his own father's lacking.

"I'll make a new batch." Dave dumped the other in the

trash. "While I'm at it, anything for the moody teen at the table?"

"Allie isn't moody," Elsie countered. "Remember? She had a rough night."

"She was crying this morning," Kacie whispered.

"I wasn't crying." Allie glared at her sisters, then her eyes shifted toward me. "I guess you didn't tell them what happened."

"No, I didn't."

"What happened?" Both girls asked in unison.

"Nothing," I said. "It's a grownup thing."

"She's not a grownup," Elsie said. "She's a teenager."

"Same difference," Allie huffed, then she turned on Dave. "Are you still pretending like you think I didn't do it?"

"Do what?" Dave asked, as if he didn't know exactly what.

"Don't play dumb, Dad." She scowled. "It never suits you."

But he was playing dumb—just as he'd warned he would upstairs. It struck me as odd.

I put myself between them. "I think your dad would rather we discuss this away from tiny, prying ears. And your dad wasn't lying yesterday. He really thinks someone staged that scene."

Dave whisked ingredients together, this time with a pinch of baking powder. He looked as if he was doing some mental calculation.

"You know what," he said. "I think I *am* going to head in to work now. We'll sort this out when I get back."

"Really? That's how you're going to play this?" My blood began to boil.

But just as fast as it started, something calming swept around me.

Magic.

Mom.

"Good morning, my favorite people." She trudged through the kitchen and motioned to take over Dave's pancake duty.

He relented his prep station and the griddle.

"All right," Mom said. "Who's helping me flip?"

Elsie and Kacie raised their hands.

I followed Dave up the stairs.

"I know you're still mad," he said. "I get it. I do. But you said it yourself. On a day like today, I'd normally go into work."

"But your head?"

"It's fine." He was a bad liar.

"Plus"—Dave looked down the stairs to the bottom where Allie was eavesdropping—"she's not going to feel any better until we catch whoever did this."

"You're right," I said. "I hate it when you're right."

13

CONSTANCE CAMPBELL AND THE VAPE SHOP CHARM

I f there was one thing I was good at, it was a crisis. Even before turning forty and becoming a witch, I'd been someone other people counted on when things got dire—and they had gotten dire.

How many foes had I stood up to since becoming a witch? How many difficult situations had I navigated?

Several.

The key was to keep my head up when under pressure.

At Dave's house, the pressure proved to be intense. The foe, a teenage girl, had sulked throughout the day. She refused to talk to me or to my mother. And her father wasn't helping matters. He was gone the entirety of the day.

When Dave returned, it was without answers to anything. They hadn't yet identified either of the bodies. They were still working on leads and gathering evidence.

The next morning, I was happy just to get out of the house. Even if it was for work—a midmorning shift at Bewitched Books, the bookstore and coffee shop I ran with my best friend Trish.

The truth was I'd never been through a crisis alone. I

had help. From Gran, from Dave, and from my witchy friends. Trish, in particular.

She was a snarky spitfire of a woman with jet black hair, save a strip she colored violet. She wore heavy eyeliner. Always dressed in black. And never kept her opinions to herself.

Most of our friends thought this new bookstore endeavor was Trish's idea. But it wasn't. Charming the vape shop to move across town was my idea.

Trish happily went along with it. Beneath October's crescent moon, we had concocted a spell to considerably remove the ever-present but nuisance shop away from our little strip mall. This was so we could realize our own dream.

The very next afternoon, a For Lease sign popped into the vape shop's window. And to be fair, they were thriving in their new facility, which neighbored Jade Gerwig's grocery store.

Once the vape shop was gone, Trish and I secured a loan. We bought the whole strip, and the building was gutted and transformed. Now, there were no dividing walls between our former unit and the old Brew at the Burrow. It was all a large and singular space.

Floor-to-ceiling bookcases lined three of the four walls. They held everything from self-help books to cookbooks and romance novels. Between bookshelves, there were comfy reading chairs where customers could sit and browse the books on display.

A small out-of-sight corner held an array of occult and paranormal items for sale. In that area, there were two locked cases that held spell books, grimoires, and other magic supplies. A glamour protected them from unwanted eyes. And for the most part, it did its job well.

Except a week ago when a contingent of *Creel Creek After Dark* fans found their way back there.

Trish was able to guide them over to a glass case against the back wall containing a few grimoires and spell books. These were fake and marked up two hundred percent—Trish's idea.

In the far corner, where Brew at the Burrow had given me my first hit of the coffee shop love, a sleek espresso machine hissed next to a refrigerated display case of tasty pastries and slices of pie. A row of barstools lined the wall beside it. Several customers sat atop them, sipping lattes with their laptops plugged into the wall sockets, one per chair.

It was quite the turnaround from its previous incarnation—a run-down used bookshop. Now, it was a thriving hub of books and coffee. Both had a splash of the paranormal thrown in. I'd revamped the latte menu to include bewitching brews like the Death by Chocolate Mocha, Charmed Caramel Latte, and Cinnamon Spelled Cold Brew.

Some things, however, never change. Trish's hair bobbed above the espresso machine. It took no less than a minute for her vivid green eyes to scan the room and find me dawdling.

"You're late," she said, so matter-of-factly I almost thought it was true.

I checked my watch. "No, you're early. Actually, I didn't think you were supposed to work today."

"I wasn't." Trish handed me a coffee cup. "But Jared called in sick. I volunteered for the early shift since my co-owner's going through a bit of a family crisis."

"Not technically a co-owner. And I wouldn't call it a family crisis."

"No?"

"No," I said. "It's more like a regular Creel Creek type crisis with a little family drama thrown in."

I stared down into the cup, surprised by what I found. Trish had made a heart with the pour of frothed milk.

Latte art? And a heart at that. Who does she think she is?

Maybe some people do change. First, she volunteers for the early shift. And now, she pours a heart into my drink. This was not the Trish I knew.

Something was off. Something was different. Good thing it wasn't my mocha, which tasted warm and creamy. The chocolatey goodness wrapped me up like a warm hug, something I hadn't received from Dave since our fight.

Back to true form, Trish rolled her eyes. "Listen. I know how you can be when dealing with crises. You don't have to be here today if you don't want to be."

"Crises?" I scowled. "No, it's like I said—the singular plain ole, everyday Creel Creek crisis. You know the kind. Bodies popping up and us solving the crime."

Trish gave me a look that said something akin to, *Oh, you poor soul. You have no idea what you're saying.*

"All right," I conceded. "Maybe there's a little more to it than that."

"There's a lot more to it," Trish said. "I know Dave didn't turn at the full moon. And I'm *not* the only one who does."

Okay... maybe I wasn't as good in a crisis as I thought.

14

TRISH HARRIS AND THE AIMLESS DETECTIVE

"I t's not as bad you think." Trish put her hands up placatingly.

But it sounded bad.

I hadn't told anyone. Dave, I was positive, hadn't told another soul.

"Who else knows?" I asked her.

We were behind the cafe counter, and every person within earshot had headphones in. A few other patrons were locked in conversation with a friend, well away from our gossip.

"My new girlfriend." Trish's green eyes seemed to gauge my reaction.

My eyes widened. But not in a bad way. Trish was always so quiet about her love-life. Over the years we'd known each other, she'd dated men *and* women. But she hardly ever told me much about them.

My curiosity about her dating life was trumped by my concern for Dave. "How?" I asked. "How does she know?"

"She's a shifter. She said she heard it through the grapevine." Trish shrugged. "I didn't really ask for specifics. I didn't think it would matter. If she knows, that means it's only a matter of time before..."

"Before what?"

"Before the whole shifter community knows. You know how they are."

"Unfortunately, I do." I sighed. "They're like one big unhappy dysfunctional family."

I still didn't understand how they'd know anything.

Unless... unless Dave told Mac and hadn't admitted as much to me.

A problem for another time.

Now, I was ready to dig deeper into Trish's love life. "When we were you going to tell me you had a new girl-friend? And what happened to your boyfriend?"

"Obviously, it didn't work out," Trish said.

"Yeah, but when did you break up?"

"About a month ago."

"And when did you meet..." I went fishing for her new girlfriend's name.

"Cassie. We met less than a month ago at one of those speed dating things. Anyway, you'd like her."

My mind was slow to catch up. "You went speed dating?"

That didn't sound like the Trish I knew.

"We all did." She rattled names off on her fingers. "Summer. Lauren. Kalene."

"You mean you had a witch's night without me?" I didn't know why I felt hurt, but it stung not to be invited.

"Uh, last I checked, you were fine in the dating department."

"I'd still like to know when you do things. I could've come along and been your wing-woman."

Trish rolled her eyes. "You would've hated every minute

of it. Trust me. But it's funny, I think we all met someone that night."

This explained the heart on my latte but left way more questions about how Dave's curse-less night leaked out to the public.

"That *is* pretty cool," I said. "Well, when do I get to meet her?"

Trish shrugged again, but this time it was playful. "Never? At least not until she's a permanent fixture. Friends and love lives don't mix well. At least, until they do. But things are awkward enough at the beginning of a relationship. I told her she's not allowed here. This is my fortress of solitude."

Except there wasn't much solitude about it.

"Ah hum." Someone fake coughed at the register.

Trish stiffened.

With a quick glance over her shoulder, I understood why.

A red-haired detective leaned against the counter. He had a slight smirk on his dumb face and a toothpick hanging loosely from his too-thin lips.

Mac.

I wondered just how long he'd been standing there and, more importantly, how much he'd overheard.

Even more importantly, had Dave told him everything about the night of the full moon?

"Detective," I said, attempting to hide my displeasure. "To what do we owe the pleasure?"

"I got an ID on that guy Dave found."

"Yeah?"

He nodded. "The guy wasn't local."

"And?" Trish joined with her own cross-examination.

Mac smiled down at her. "The last place he visited in Creel Creek was here."

"That's all very interesting," Trish said. "I'm still not sure why you're here."

Mac seemed to feed off Trish's displeasure. "Trish," he said, "let's you and me have a chat in the private room, okay?"

"What about me?" I asked.

"No, Constance, you weren't working at the time."

"Still, I might be able to help."

"Actually, you can help," Mac said. "I'd love a cup of coffee and a slice of pie."

The way he said it, I knew he wasn't expecting to pay for them.

I poured him a cup of our plain Jane drip coffee, spelled it to a nice lukewarm, then cut the thinnest sliver of chocolate pie.

Mac took them without a thank you.

Instead, he had other words of wisdom. "I know you like to insert yourself into our investigations. And Dave told me not to let you get involved this time. See, but I know how you ladies operate. Anything I tell her, she'll tell you."

Trish snorted. "Is that your long-winded way of saying she can come along?" She turned to me. "Get your booty in there while I find someone to cover the cafe."

Mac shrugged in agreement. He took his coffee and pie through the seating area to where a barn door opened into an intimate meeting space.

Typically, the door was open to the rest of the store, but Mac closed it behind us.

Inside, the room had a large oak table and firm office chairs. It was roomy enough for small gatherings between friends but nothing more.

"Something's up with Dave, huh?" Mac took a seat and admired the spread of pie and coffee before him. He scooped a small bite of pie onto his fork.

"What makes you say that?" A better detective might notice the worry etched on my face, but Mac was too busy with the pie.

"He just seems a little off," Mac said. "Not himself. I don't know. I'm probably reading too much into it. It'd spook the hell out of me if someone tried to frame me for murder. And between us, I can't even fathom a curse like his. Shifters like me have control. We control when we change and every action we take while we're changed. A full moon comes around and he loses all control. It isn't fair."

So he *didn't* know about Dave's night.

"No, it's not," I agreed.

"Funny thing though, there was a footprint over by the campsite. Smaller than Dave's. Come to that, smaller than yours. Was anyone out there with you when you dropped Dave off?"

"Why? Do you think it's important?"

"Could be. Could be the killer's. That is, unless someone was with you."

How had Mac gotten so quickly to the point without me seeing it coming? Maybe he was a better detective than I thought.

I had to think quickly. I was at a crossroads. If I lied now, there'd be no turning back.

Or I could tell him the truth—that it must be Allie's footprint—but I'd still be leaving important information out.

Omissions are lies.

"It might be Allie's print," I said. "She went up there with me."

"Huh." Mac took a sip of lukewarm coffee. "She's the oldest, right? How old is she, now?"

He made a face as the coffee went down his throat.

I was about to answer him when Trish slid the door open and barreled into the room. "All right. I'm here. What can we do to help?"

"Trish." Mac lost his focus. "Hold on a second. Let me dig up my notes." Mac flipped to a page in his little black notebook. "I need a list of who all was working last Tuesday."

Trish sat down beside me. "I don't know off the top of my head, but that's not a problem. I can get you that information."

"Fair enough," Mac said. "And I'll want to speak to each of them separately."

"About?" Trish's green eyes narrowed.

"About what they saw on Tuesday... if anything."

Trish flipped some stray hair behind her ear, then shook her head. "If we allow you to talk to our staff during the workday, then you're going to have to dish something to us. After all, we gave you the pie."

"What do you want to know?"

"Who died?" she asked.

"I told you he wasn't local. Name's Tyson Briggs. Twenty-six years old. From around Richmond. We contacted his next-of-kin earlier today. Haven't really pieced together why he was in Creel Creek in the first place. But I have a hunch it had something to do with this bookstore."

"Why would it have anything to do with us?"

"I know what kind of books you keep in that dark corner."

"How much did he spend here?" Trish asked.

"What?" Mac's brow furrowed.

"How much did he spend here? I can tell you if he bought a book."

Mac looked down at his notes. "Five dollars and sixty-three cents."

"A medium signature latte," Trish and I said in near unison.

"What's that?" Mac reached for his notepad.

"Either the Death by Chocolate Mocha or the Charmed Caramel Latte," Trish answered. "Any other medium latte is about twenty cents cheaper. And the large is, well, it's more. And the pie is about fifty cents less."

"So, he didn't buy a book," I said.

Mac raised a shoulder. "Maybe you didn't have what he was looking for."

"Is this how you always do things?" I asked him. "There's a lot of speculation here. What actually do you know?"

"Well, now I know he bought a medium signature latte. Do you think any of your baristas might remember making this drink, say around 3:00 PM that day?"

"Doubtful," Trish said.

"Really?" Mac's near permanent smirk became a frown. "You speak for everyone?"

"No," she answered. "I speak for myself. I made the latte, so I doubt if any of our baristas are going to remember doing it."

"You made the drink?" Mac took another sip of his coffee. His face puckered.

Not warm enough.

"I do work here," Trish said.

"Yeah, well, do you remember the guy you made it for? What was he doing here? Who was he with? I've got a photo of him if it'll help."

Trish's eyes reached high into her skull. "Why didn't you start with that?"

"We're all headed to the same destination," Mac said. "So what if I take the long way around."

"I'm not much for scenic," Trish quipped. "We have customers waiting. This is our business. We'd like to keep it running."

"And this is my business." Mac slid a photo across the table. It was of a handsome young man with brown hair and a charming smile. Dimples lit up both sides of his cheeks. "Do you remember Tyson Briggs or not?"

"I do," Trish said slowly. "He was part of that group."

"What group?" Mac asked.

Trish huffed. "Some *Creel Creek After Dark* weirdos. They caused a bit of a stir."

Mac clicked a pen and brought it scratching down in his notebook. "What happened?"

"Nothing much. They ordered some drinks and were here in this room for a while together. But then they snuck into the corner you mentioned—the corner with the spell books. How they got past my charm on it, I don't know."

"I told you, I had a hunch," Mac said.

"Yeah, well, I stopped them before they got into real trouble."

Mac stopped his scribbling. "If that's the case, Trish, then tell me—why'd this guy end up dead?"

15

CONSTANCE CAMPBELL AND
THE LUMP

I spent the next few days worried my truth would spell trouble for Allie, for Dave, and probably least on my list—but still a priority—me.

Was Mac going to show up on our doorstep with handcuffs? I thought so with every car that zoomed through the neighborhood and when the delivery drivers dropped off their packages.

But it never happened.

Maybe my words hadn't meant as much to the detective as I thought.

And even weirder, Mac's throwaway words had stuck with me. "He seems a little off," Mac had said about Dave.

But Mac was wrong. Dave wasn't just a little off. He wasn't himself.

When he was home, he didn't enjoy the same things. He'd stopped reading the book beside his bed. He hardly talked to me or the girls. He got angry, with the tiniest of things setting him off.

That was when he was there. But he wasn't home much.

He didn't eat with us. He came home late and one night, not at all.

So, I was surprised when Dave showed up at Bewitched Books. It was the end of my shift. He was in his uniform, and he asked if I wanted to help him out with something to do with the case.

"What is it?" I asked, knowing I was going to say yes regardless.

"They identified the *other* body," Dave said. "Turns out, a man was reported missing several years back—when I was a teenager, I mean. They were able to find some dental records. Everything matched up. I'm going to notify the widow now. I don't know if I can do it alone."

"You won't have to." I scooped up my purse from behind the counter.

He smiled into a nod.

I followed Dave's SUV to the main highway. The familiar road led out of town to the vineyard, then to a long stretch of miles before Charlottesville.

But we weren't going that far. We turned onto a utility road shortly after the county hospital. Numerous doctor offices, outpatient surgery centers, and a few dentists took up residence on each side of the road.

I assumed the road circled back around to the hospital, but I was wrong. The street dead-ended at a prominent building. The signage read, *Creel Creek Commons: an assisted living facility specializing in memory care.*

The dreaded term "memory care." With a sinking feeling in my chest, I wondered if the widow would remember her missing husband.

This task could be impossible—notifying a loved one of something that happened so long in the past when they couldn't remember the past.

We made our way to the reception area and signed in. Then we navigated around an old woman in the hallway tiptoeing around with her wheelchair like it was a Flint-stone's car.

She wasn't the only resident out and about. The hall-ways were filled with others, each of them looking at us expectantly, as if maybe we were there to see them. There were hopeful glints but no recognition in their eyes.

Some of the hallway doors were decorated, either by family or the residents themselves. Some had wreaths and ribbons. Some done up big. Some small. They were almost like the outside of a house, each door showing the person-ality of the occupant within.

Or the lack of.

For every door with a little pizzazz, there were at least three others without. Most of them wide open with a view of the room inside.

The place made me feel sad. These people, while there were so many in close proximity, were each alone. Most kept to themselves, choosing to watch TV in their room instead of socializing with others.

A family was congregated in a day room, the small chil-dren too trepidatious to approach their grandmother.

Along the way, Dave kept repeating the room number, as if we'd both forget.

We passed through some fire doors into what had to be the back wing of the building. The widow's room was at the very end of the corridor. The door was as beige and blank as it could be.

Not a good sign.

Dave faltered. "Look," he said. "There's a solid chance we're wasting our time here."

"You don't know that. Regardless, she needs to know what happened to him."

"I don't plan on telling her the details," Dave said, then rapped lightly on the door.

"Come in." A raspy voice sounded on the other side.

Dave nudged the door wide. I guessed, like me, he'd seen the inside of enough rooms to be wary. It could be octogenarian and X-rated. No telling what parts of this woman were exposed.

I was relieved the answer was none.

The bed in the middle of the room was empty, and it was made up with tight corners. A multicolor Afghan was folded neatly at the end.

"I'll be out in a second." Again, the voice came from behind a closed door—this time the bathroom.

Aside from the bed, the room was furnished sparsely with a recliner, a wooden chair in the corner, a television on the wall, a nightstand, a dresser, and a mini fridge rounding it out.

Row after row of knickknacks lined the top of her dresser—framed pictures, hairbrushes, a tin of hard candy, and several random pieces of jewelry. There was a pearl necklace, diamond earrings, and a bracelet with several charms—a butterfly, half a heart, and a moon.

"They're fake." The woman burst out of the bathroom. "Everything I own is fake. That way it's less apt to get stolen. Mind you, it still does from time to time. But I don't cry over stainless-steel junk like I did silver."

Dave cleared his throat. "Are you Maude Jenkins?"

"Last time I checked," she said. "Who are you? The police? You've finally come to hear me out about the gross man next door?"

"What gross man?" I asked.

"He assaulted me," she said, animated. "Grabbed my fanny on the way to BINGO!"

A nurse strode inside the already cramped space with a rolling blood pressure monitor. "Arthur's been dead for a year now, Mrs. Jenkins."

Maude frowned. "They still might want to hear about it."

"I assure you they do not." The nurse eyed Dave's name tag. "Do you, Sheriff Marsters? Wait. Does that really mean you're the sheriff?"

"Afraid so," Dave said.

Maude was a thin, frail woman. Her skin hung loosely on her cheeks and neck. She wore a matching shirt and pant combo, all sea-foam green. Her glasses were large and square, covering most of her face in a glare from the setting sun out the room's window.

Not really sitting but hovering above the Afghan, the old woman resigned herself to the nurse's vital checks.

"Where's Emily?" she asked.

The nurse strapped a cuff to Maude's arm. "It's Emily's day off."

"Already?"

"Believe it or not, we get two days off every week." The nurse smirked. Her own name tag read Jennifer in fine print. "Honestly, Mrs. Jenkins, what does the sheriff want with you?"

"If you stop your blabbering, maybe we can find out." Maude's tiny black eyes found Dave. "Now, what brings you here today, Sheriff?"

"It can wait," Dave said. "You might prefer some privacy."

Maude shook her head. "I haven't had privacy in nine

years. Not since my daughter stuck me in this place and left town. Go ahead, ask how many times she's come to visit."

"I'd rather not." Dave's neck went red and blotchy.

"Never," Maude answered. "She never visits."

"I'm sorry to hear that," I said.

"No." She waved it off. "It's fine. We never got on anyway. Oh, and by the way, who exactly are you?"

"I'm, uh, Constance... a friend of the sheriff."

Friend?

"What is it with young people these days?" Maude asked. "Emily's always talking about her friend too. Call a spade a spade, why don't you? If he's your boyfriend or if he's your lover, just say so."

"He's both," I told her.

"There. Was that so hard?"

"No. It wasn't." I smiled, but it quickly faded as I recalled the grim reason we were there.

"Okay, Sheriff. I guess introductions are over. Hit me with your best shot."

Dave tugged at his collar. The room was a little warm, but it had to be Maude's indifferent attitude putting him off.

"I'm almost done," Jennifer said. "Besides, I don't think they want me in here when they charge you for those heinous crimes you committed."

"What crime is that?" I asked.

The nurse shrugged. "Just joking. I'll see you next week, Mrs. Jenkins. Emily will be back tomorrow."

"Good!" Maude rubbed at the place the cuff had been. "Emily's the nurse who takes care of me most of the time. I like her the best. She talks to me like we're family. No one else treats me like that."

"I heard that," Jennifer said, leaving the room.

"I'm sorry," I said again.

"You keep saying that like it's true." Maude sighed. "Maybe you are sorry, but I'm not asking you to be. I would like to know why you're here though. And why you do the talking while the sheriff over there acts like a lump."

"I'm not a lump," Dave argued.

"Prove it," she said. "Say what you came to say."

"Uh, yeah," Dave began. "Mrs. Jenkins—"

"Call me Maude."

"Maude," he repeated, his hand on his collar again. "We have some news about your husband."

"News?" The old woman's frown lines deepened. "What kind of news?"

"Well, he's dead," Dave answered her. "His body was found about a week ago."

"I thought you said you had news? That's not news. I've known he was dead for thirty years. So has the insurance company that tried to get out of paying me."

"But this confirms it." Dave released his hold on his collar. He seemed to struggle for what to say next.

So, I jumped in. "Maude, can you tell us what happened when he went missing?"

"What happened?" Maude got up from the bed, turning her back to us as she shuffled over to the recliner. "Nothing much happened. He went camping one weekend, and he never came back."

"What kind of camping?"

"The regular kind," Maude said. "Frank was an outdoorsy type. Hunting. Fishing. I swear he just liked to get away from me. That and he liked to make instant coffee and piss in the woods—in that order. Personally, I can't stand the stuff, and I hate pissing in the woods."

I eyed Dave. Surely, he would ask her something. When

he didn't, I continued my line of questioning. "So, you never went with Frank?"

"Not if I could help it. My daughter though—she loved it. It's a miracle she wasn't with him that weekend."

"Why do you say that?"

"Cause I'm guessing she'd have ended up dead too." Maude made a show of turning on the television. It came on with the volume blaring some news program. She spoke over it. "Do you know what happened to him? To Frank. What killed him?"

"We're working on it," Dave said.

Maude pressed a button, and the chair began to recline, the footrest folding out.

Figuring I'd worn out my welcome, I waited for Dave to say something, but he was looking expectantly over at me.

"Did they recover any of his things?" I asked. "His tent? His gear? Anything?"

"If they did, they didn't return them to me," Maude said. "Why do you ask? And again, why are you asking so many questions?"

"I'm just here to help."

"Your boyfriend's being a lump again," Maude said.

"I don't think he's met many spitfires like you."

"Fair enough," she said. "I've been told I can be a handful." She didn't exactly dismiss us, but her attention went to the television.

I was at a loss, unsure what else to ask or say. And Dave —he was being a lump. I motioned my head toward the door.

He nodded. "Thank you for your time," he told Maude. "If you have any questions or if you need to talk about any of this, you can reach out." Dave handed her his card.

"I'll have to call my daughter," Maude said. "I'm guessing

she'll want another funeral. We didn't have the body last time."

Dave nodded. "She can arrange that once the remains are released."

"Thank you, Sheriff." Maude's hard stare fell on me. "And thank you, Constance. Not sure he'd have got the words out if you weren't here to coax them."

Dave chuckled, then we said our goodbyes and left the room.

We retraced our steps through the maze of hallways, finally reaching the reception desk. Jennifer, the nurse who had checked Maude's vitals, was there with a Styrofoam cup of coffee in hand.

"Is everything okay with Mrs. Jenkins?" she asked.

"Fine," Dave said. "And don't worry. She's not in any trouble."

"I didn't figure." She laughed. "Maude hates it when I tease her."

"I have a question for you," I said.

"Shoot."

"Is Maude lucid like that all the time?"

"Mrs. Jenkins?" She smiled. "Oh, for sure. Her memory's fine. You saw she can be a bit of a pill, but I guess every resident is like that in their own way. In fact, Mrs. Jenkins could be living on her own if it wasn't for her episodes."

"Episodes?"

"It's nothing really," the nurse reassured. "Just a tantrum or two every month. Sometimes we have to strap her down to the bed."

"Really?" Dave's brow furrowed.

Jennifer blinked slowly, as if she'd revealed too much information. "We know it's not ideal. But honestly, she's more a danger to herself than anyone else."

I'd heard that phrase many times before. Like every other time, I doubted its validity—because the truth is people hurt each other a lot more often than they hurt themselves.

16

THE WITCHES

Every month, our group of witches got together, not to spell or charm, nor to brew potions, but to simply commune with each other.

To shoot the proverbial not nice word.

This was typically a morning meeting of the minds accompanied by the greatest elixir known to mankind—coffee. But sometimes plans changed, mornings became night, and we communed with wine, which also held a spot in my top five beverages. Not that I could name the other three.

Today's meeting couldn't have come at a better time.

It was our first meeting at Bewitched Books for nearly two months—since the big renovation.

Most of the others—Lauren Whittaker, Kalene Moone, and Summer Shields—were inside taking it all in.

In turns, they meandered over through the charmed section, then out to the romance section on the other side. I watched as Kalene grabbed several books with man chest on the covers and stuck them under her arm.

She brought them to my register and ordered drinks for

everyone. Then Lauren and Summer wandered through the cafe to the back room.

"It's about that time," I told Trish, discarding my apron and waving to Jared to take over for me.

"Yeah, yeah, I'm coming." Trish was busy organizing a stack of boxes for the mailman to pick up.

I nodded and headed over to meet the other witches.

As I entered the cramped room, a mixture of coffee and other scents hit me like a sucker punch to the nostrils. Lauren, our potion master, had been brewing that morning. The soft smell of woodsmoke hovered close to her curly brown hair. She greeted me with a smile, her big blue eyes gleaming in the vintage lighting.

A Sputnik chandelier thrust Edison bulbs in all directions above the darkly stained table.

Next to Lauren was Kalene. She was short and frumpy with a braid of long hair that hung past the waistband of her faded jeans. She wore cowboy boots with—if my nose wasn't mistaken—horse manure caked on the bottom.

Summer Shields took a seat opposite the others, leaving me to sit either with her or at the head or foot of the table.

Summer had pointed features and red hair that could only be found in a bottle. Her perfume mixed with another scent.

"Were you burning incense?" I asked, sitting beside her.

"Jade was." She rolled her eyes. "We're working on ideas for the next episode. Sorry about the last one, by the way. I tried to steer the topic away from Dave but—"

"She wasn't having it," I said. "I know how Jade is. Once she sinks her teeth into something, she's not letting go."

"Is that a werewolf joke?" She smirked into a big gulp of coffee.

"It was," I said. "And he's the only werewolf in town, so a

scene like that—there's only going to be one conclusion to sink her fangs into."

Even though I didn't mean to throw it in, Summer picked up on my sarcasm. "You say that like it's not true?"

"That's because it's not." Trish strode into the room, a teacup in one hand and a slice of pumpkin pie in the other. She took the spot at the head of the table and shrugged at us through the glares. "What? I didn't have breakfast."

"It's not about the pie," Summer said. "Although it looks good. We want to know what you and Constance seem to know that the rest of us don't. What do you mean Dave isn't the only werewolf in town? He is, right?"

"Honestly, ladies. The whole store can hear you." With a waggle of Trish's finger, the barn door between us and the café slid closed.

"It is kind of annoying," Lauren said to the room, but her words were meant for me. "You always tell Trish stuff long before us. We have a group text for a reason."

"I couldn't say this in a text," I argued.

"To tell the truth, my death stare *was* about the pie," Kalene interrupted me. "But Lauren's right. Why does Trish get to hear everything first? She wasn't even part of the Faction."

Summer's whole face puckered. "The Faction was never real."

"It felt real." Kalene withdrew from the argument with a whisper.

"Can we all just take a chill pill?" With another wave of her hand, Trish sent a wave of magic throughout the room. A calming energy settled in my chest, and I imagined every other person felt it too.

"Using magic on us?" Summer snorted a laugh. "I thought that's against the rules."

"Eh." Trish shrugged. "It's not like we're at Hogwarts."

"I don't approve of it." Lauren tilted her head, her big blue eyes filled with a dreamy glaze. "But I don't not approve either."

"Look what you've done to her," Kalene said. "She can barely do words anymore."

"I'm not convinced any of you can do words." Trish took a bite of pie. "Besides, today we're here for Constance. I'll let her run the show."

"I never said I wanted to make this meeting about me."

"You never want to," Trish said. "It just happens. And we're always here for you anyway—even when we feel left out. Right, Lauren? Kalene? I'm guessing neither of you have anything more pressing than a couple of bodies found in the woods?"

"Not unless you count that I'm dating again," Lauren said. "I think you might remember how much of a fiasco it turned out to be the last time I tried."

"Yeah, well, we all have our ghosts, don't we?" Trish's father was a haunting spirit we hoped to never see again.

"What about you, Kalene?"

"Uh, I'm dating someone too. But I'm not sure it's relevant to this conversation."

"Congratulations." Trish forked another scoop of pie. "And for everyone's information, I'm also dating. If you bring it up again, I'll curse you. There, Constance—see how easy it is to derail the conversation into fluffy nonsense? Wouldn't you rather be discussing your crisis?"

"I'd rather not have a crisis," I said.

"I'll bite," Summer said. "Sorry. That was a poor choice of words. What I mean is what's going on? What don't we already know about the werewolf situation?"

"A lot," I said and gave them a rundown of what

happened to Dave, finding Allie, and finally the two bodies in the woods.

"Mac was in here the other day. Looks like the first victim was a fan of your show," Trish told Summer.

"What kind of fan?"

Trish raised a shoulder. "He was in here with a group of others. I overheard them talking about the show. Later, they barged into the restricted section."

"Oh." Summer absentmindedly raked her fingers through her hair. "Did they come out bald or what?"

"I ushered them out of there before it came to that. But it makes me wonder..."

"Wonder what?" Summer asked.

"If one of them did it. Or all of them. You know how crazy that wannabe paranormal crowd gets."

Trish still held a grudge from our quasi-captivity at After Dark Con. I couldn't really blame her.

"Since when did you become the investigative type?" Summer asked her, a hint of a gleam in her eyes.

"Since Mac showed up here unannounced and blamed my store as a motive for the murder."

"Oh?" Summer's eyes ping-ponged between me and Trish, finally landing on me. "So, I take it Dave's not working the case?"

"He's not," I told her. "He's been relegated to other tasks. Granted, I don't know how well he'd work this case anyway. He hasn't been himself lately—not since that night."

"You mean the night he didn't turn?" Kalene finally caught up in the conversation.

"That's the night." Trish rolled her eyes.

Lauren perked up. "Does Mac know about Allie—that she's a werewolf?"

I shook my head.

"Oh." Her eyes darted away from mine, and she drummed her fingers against her coffee cup.

"I know—I know it's bad." I sighed. "That's why I didn't want to tell you. I hate lying."

Omissions are lies.

"You can tell us anything," Kalene offered. "We're on your side, no matter what."

"We'll help," Lauren added.

"I'll do some digging," Summer said. "After all, digging's what I do best." Wincing, she covered her mouth with a hand. "Sorry. Also, not the best use of words. I'll shut up now."

"You do that," Trish said.

Then she turned her attention on me, her eyes narrowed. "What exactly did you mean when you said Dave's not himself?"

17

THE OTHER SIDE

OTHER DAVE

A t first, I thought it was a dream. Then I realized it was. It was *the dream*—the dream I'd had since I'd popped into existence. And the dream I was sure I'd never see again.

Not after the last time I escaped the mental prison of Dave's mind.

But he was quicker then. Quick of wit and strong of will. When it happened, when he realized his mistake, he put a swift end to my newfound freedoms.

I thanked the Moon for the mishap that enabled this escape.

Still, with each passing day, I feared being put back there.

Back into the darkness once again.

"I'm not going back there. Not this time." Even after several days, the words still sounded strange to my ears.

But it wasn't the words that were a problem. The words

came easy. Too easy. Somehow, I knew everything he knew. I had his memories, too. They mingled with mine.

It was his voice. I couldn't get used to it.

I thought I should sound meaner.

Sounding mean was one thing. I didn't want to be meaner.

"I plan to be better this time," I told the mirror. "Not just in behavior. That too. But I'll be better prepared for your tricks."

You know you can keep your thoughts to yourself, right? You don't have to keep speaking them aloud.

I grunted. "Easy for you to say. It might be easier if someone else wasn't taking up so much space in my thoughts."

They're my thoughts!

In the fogged mirror of the bathroom, Dave's reflection stared back at me with cold, dark eyes. I guess it was my reflection too. I flexed each muscle. Not trying to be vain, more the opposite.

"You're so fleshy," I told him. "So weak."

It was hard to comprehend how someone like Dave could maintain control over something like me.

Dave had put me in a box a long time ago. I wasn't allowed out to play. Not without the full moon as a backdrop. That was when he disappeared. That was when I overpowered him like the weakling I knew he was.

I don't know how you did this, but it needs to stop now. There's too much on the line. I can't allow you to stay on the loose like this.

"Allow me?" I laughed hardily. "Dave, my good boy—and you are a good boy—you aren't in control. Not anymore."

It's only a matter of time before you lose control.

I allowed his comment to stew. To fester. "Lose control? Lose control how?"

You know how.

"No, Dave. I don't know what you mean. Do you mean lose control of your body? Of your mind? Or do you mean lose control in the literal sense?"

I meant the former. But if you do lose control... if you go on a rampage, hurt anyone... I swear I'll... I'll...

"You'll do nothing because you're in there and I'm out here." I smiled at the mirror, my teeth gleaming, if a little less sharp than I was used to. "If I understand the concept correctly—and I think I do—we're like the ends of magnets. What are they called?"

Polar opposites.

"Right. Exactly. How we're communicating now, I don't understand it. And I wish it to stop."

Then make it stop. Go back to where you belong. Leave my family alone.

"I don't belong there, in the darkness. At least not anymore." I gritted Dave's—my—teeth. "I'm not going to hurt your family. Don't you forget, they're my family too. You'd understand that if you ever listened to Dad."

I spent too long listening to that old man. Look where it's got me. Look where it got us. He's to blame for all of this.

"Maybe." I shrugged. "Maybe not. You never know. It's possible he was set up too."

You're dreaming.

"You're right about that." I threw on Dave's uniform shirt. "I'm going to need your help on this case."

How about you let me out, and I solve it?

"No. I like my way better."

Course you would.

I put on Dave's uniform pants, then I strapped on his belt with its holster.

Listen. Dave's voice was pleading now. *Whatever you do with this case, don't let Constance get involved. Or rather, any more involved.*

"Relax," I said. "We visited some old lady. Nothing dangerous about it."

You don't know Constance like I do. She has a habit of putting herself into dangerous situations.

"She's a witch. She can defend herself."

It doesn't mean she's always able to. Magic is finicky. Look at what's it done here, to us.

"I see your point," I said. "Fine. I'll keep her out of harm's way. The link is strong with her. I felt it as soon as I laid eyes on her. I know you do too. It's almost like it was with—"

Don't you speak her name!

Even though I was in control, there was no reason to push. Not in that way. "I won't," I told Dave. "But I notice you haven't—"

Don't do this. You have no right, no say in my love life.

"No, Dave. You have no right. No right to exclude me from everything. Now the shoe is on the other foot. I can close you off like you do with me."

You don't know how.

"I think I do—"

I can help, Dave pleaded.

I shook my head. "You took away my freedom. We could be fine together, you know. Why—why do you always lock me away?"

Because you're reckless. Because I'm reckless when I let you have any part of my thoughts.

I could feel his emotions welling up. They were the mirror opposite of mine. "I remember the days after she passed," I said. "It wasn't me who was reckless. It wasn't me who raged."

That's not how it happened. You got free because of my mental state—the walls I'd built, they crumbled.

"Or you wanted me out. You set me free as an excuse for your own bad behavior. You set me free so you could blame me."

Not true.

"You know what," I said to the mirror. "I'm done with you, Dave. *Other* Dave. You just go ahead—watch as I steal your life."

18

CONSTANCE CAMPBELL AND THE OTHER BOYFRIEND

"I'm sure it's going to be fine." Lauren patted my back. "Dave will be back to himself in no time."

Kalene and Summer agreed with nods while Trish kept her opinions to herself.

Their words were kind and reassuring, but they weren't what I needed.

I needed answers.

But none of them had ever dated a werewolf.

When I tried to explain about Dave's *other* side—the side that he himself had trouble explaining to me—I was met with vacant stares, questions, and more vacant stares.

Kalene tried to pull information from her romance novels, and Summer took inspiration from movies. But there was nothing alpha about Dave's current behavior. If anything, he'd lost his confidence. That and we could only gain so much insight from *An American Werewolf in London*.

His hair was perfect.

As the coffee drained from each cup, the witches ran out of reasons to stay. One by one, they left. It was back to work for Trish and me.

With a twirl of her finger, she straightened up the room. Cups floated to the trash can. The crumbs swept themselves off the table, disappearing into nothingness as they crashed into the floor. The chairs scooted neatly under the table.

"New cleaning charm. What do you think?" Trish brushed her hands together, as if it had been hard work.

"Nifty." I shrugged.

In the cafe, I settled behind the counter, but I wasn't there long. Three customers in a row started toward me, then each of them veered away suddenly before making it to the register, as if they'd decided against another jolt of caffeine.

I couldn't help but discreetly take a sniff of my armpits. But everything was in order there. I smelled faintly of Secret's fresh scent mixed ever-so-slightly with Dave's favorite fabric softener.

"It's your face," Trish said. Her own was unreadable. If she was joking, I couldn't tell.

"Well, that's not very nice."

"You know what I mean." She rolled her eyes. "It's the worry etched across it. No one wants forced interaction with someone who looks so frazzled and frail."

"I don't look—" I stopped as I found my reflection in the shiny metal of the espresso machine.

"You, out! I got this." Trish shoved a hip through the swinging door and into the cramped space with me, then she sent me packing to the backroom for the remainder of my shift.

With a spelled-together website, the bookshop did a decent bit of business online. If only the spell made packing labels and stuffed spell books into boxes or padded envelopes. Magic being magic, it didn't go that far.

So, I printed out the orders and put together fifty packages before the deliveryman came to take them away. He had nearly as many in return. With the store's growth, Trish's summoning spell had grown too. Books from all over the world found their way to Bewitched Books, either when their owners passed away or were done using them.

I thanked the delivery man, then dug into the new pile. I opened a small package, allowing its contents to fall out onto the desk. Unsurprisingly, it was a book. But unlike most others, it wasn't faded or torn, nor was it leather-bound and old.

It was a new book.

I read the cover. *102 Love Potions:* An amended edition of my mother's classic *101 Love Potions* with updated ingredients, more concise language, and an additional potion by me, the author, Sheila Rae Day.

Not everything the spell summoned was gold. Knowing Trish would never stock a book of love potions—even brand new—I tossed it into the "important books bin" with several others.

"Ouch!" A small tenor voice filtered into my head. At the same time, through my ears, I heard the squeak of a mouse.

"Twinkie?" I scooped Trish's mouse familiar from the bottom of the bin. "What are you doing in there?"

"If you must know, I was reading a little smut."

"What kind of smut?" I didn't recall throwing any romance novels in the trash.

"Sex Spells and the Charms of Copulation," she answered.

"Never heard of that one." But like Twinkie, it piqued my interest. Were there really spells about love making? Or was love making part of the ritual? I could see it both ways.

"Trish threw it out yesterday," Twinkie said. *"And she forbade me from looking at it."*

"So, naturally, you had to."

"*Of course. What kind of familiar would I be if I didn't try to expand my knowledge?*"

"The kind who listens to their witch," I said. But I didn't mean it harshly. Twinkie knew my and Brad's relationship had been on the rocks for over a year now—ever since I learned he'd abandoned Mom when she'd needed him most.

I fished around the bin and found the aforementioned book. It had a dusty leather cover with what looked to be some ancient symbol on the front. Upon further study, it was something else entirely.

"No one is this flexible," I said.

"*You'd be surprised,*" Twinkie argued. "*I've seen a lot of things in my time.*"

"Gross." I made a face.

But her words had struck a chord. Like Brad and Stevie, Gran's familiar, Twinkie had been around for centuries. I couldn't help but wonder if she'd known many werewolves in that time, and if so, would she know what was happening with Dave?

"*Ask the questions, Constance. I can't answer so many at once.*"

Even though she wasn't my familiar, Twinkie could read my thoughts if she was looking into my eyes. Her beady black eyes bore into me.

"It's Dave," I said. "He's acting odd."

"*After his ordeal the other night, I wouldn't expect otherwise,*" she said. "*He's bound to be grumpy. A little antsy. A little rash. But I'm guessing that isn't what you mean, is it?*"

"He is all of those things," I said. "But no. I'm wondering about his other side. Do you happen to know what he means by that?"

"*I think I do, yeah.*" The mouse perched on its hind legs. "*I'm sure you've heard of the concept of the reptilian brain.*"

I nodded for her to go on.

"*The oldest—the base layer of evolution—where humans are at their most primal. The lizard brain is dominated by instinct and impulse, not rational thought. Its focus is on its survival.*"

I continued nodding. I took a 101-level psychology class in college.

"*Let's just say, Dave's wolf brain isn't much different.*"

"Okay. But how does that explain what's happening to him?" I asked.

"*It doesn't. Maybe you're asking the wrong questions.*"

I ignored her remark. "When he told me about it, he didn't call it his wolf brain. He called it the *other* guy. Like he has some whole other side of himself that's locked away until he becomes the wolf."

"*That's exactly what it is,*" Twinkie said. "*But think of it like this—it's the personality he developed with his wolf brain. It's the Mr. Hyde to his Dr. Jekyll.*"

"Then it can't be that. I've talked to him. I've kissed him. He's been with the girls. It can't be the Hyde.

"*Why not?*"

"Because he isn't tearing them to pieces or anything like that. He isn't a monster."

"*That's right. He's not. But he is when he's the wolf.*"

"No." I shook my head. "I don't think this is it. It's still Dave in there. He's just grumpy and withdrawn." Twinkie made a squeak. I continued over her. "If he were the wolf, I think I'd know. There'd be signs... more signs."

"*Think about it this way, Constance. When he's the wolf, he only has access to the wolf brain—to the instincts. As Dave, and I mean regular human Dave, he'll have access to everything. To the part of the brain that Dave uses to speak and for rational thoughts. He'll even have access to Dave's memories. And everything else in that complicated structure between your ears."*

I was still shaking my head, although I wasn't sure I necessarily disagreed. "How though? How can this personality—this *other* him—get out like this? And if it has, are we even able to know it?"

For the first question, I'm not sure. It could be the combination of the potions. Or something as simple as a curse. And for the second, well, we'll find out soon enough."

I shot her a questioning look.

"*Dave's here,*" she said. "*Trish just sent him our way.*"

I leaned back in the chair, trying to get a vantage to the storefront. I could just make out lights and shapes through the crack between the two-way doors. But there was nothing definitive.

Then a silhouette blocked out the overhead lights in the cafe.

I craned my neck a little farther. When I did, the chair became unsteady and rocked backward toward the hard ground.

Without thinking, without uttering a spell aside from a hasty curse, a jolt of magic shot down from my spine to my fingertips. Both the chair and my body hovered a few inches from the floor.

The doors swung open.

Dave couldn't have timed his entry any better had he planned it.

DAVE LINGERED IN THE DOORWAY, hesitant to step any closer.

Not that I'd blame him. I was splayed out, nearly

touching the floor, and being held aloft by a magic spell I wasn't in control of.

"I was going to ask if this was a good time to chat, but I can already see it's not."

"One second," I huffed before muttering a quick spell. The chair righted itself in a motion reminiscent of a carnival ride. My insides somersaulted.

"Are you sure you're okay?"

"Fine," I said.

Dave looked the same as he always did. His uniform was a tad wrinkled, as if he'd taken it out of a cold dryer. He filled it out well enough.

But there was something different there. The circles beneath his eyes were a dark purple. His five o'clock shadow was thicker than usual, more akin to a beard than his typical mustache and stubble.

I couldn't glean anything from appearance. What he was hiding was on the inside, and only Twinkie could see in there.

Dave was, and he'd always been, a man who kept his emotions in check. He was unreadable.

Until now, he'd always let me in.

Part of me wanted to grab him by the waist and kiss him, as if that kiss would give me the truth I desired. Another part of me, a much bigger part, wanted to run away.

"What was that all about?" Dave made a motion like the chair acrobatics.

"Oh, that? I was just, uh, practicing some magic." I was not a good liar.

"So, that's what you do for fun these days." He smiled, but there was no sincerity behind it. This conversation was starting out stilted and off, just like I thought Dave was.

"That's a lot of packages." He pointed to the delivery pile. "Are there really so many witches out there?"

"Why do you ask?" My tone wasn't nearly as light as I meant it to sound. *Think, Constance. Think.* "Are you looking to trade me in?"

Why is talking to him so hard?

"*Because you're overthinking it,*" Twinkie said. "*Calm down. Pretend it's really him, and I'll get a look inside his head.*"

Right. Calm.

"Nah." Dave—if it was really him—chuckled. "I think I'll keep you around a while."

"A while?" I arched an eyebrow. I don't know why I said it. Maybe because if it was really Dave, I liked to see his reactions to silly things like this. It was fun to watch him squirm.

This Dave didn't squirm.

"You know what I mean," he said flatly.

"I might," I told him. "Besides, that was kind of a trap with no suitable answer."

"I don't like being trapped." Dave's tone was harsh, but after a moment, his features softened. "Sorry." He pinched the bridge of his nose. "It's been a long day."

"Same here."

"Yeah?" He crinkled his forehead and gazed at me through dark brown eyes. In that moment, I could see him —my Dave.

Maybe I was wrong about all of this.

Maybe I'd let Trish get in my head.

"Anything you need to tell me about?" he asked.

I smiled. "Sure. That is, if you want to hear about the love lives of our local witches."

He smiled back. "You know, I think I'll pass."

It was Dave's smile I'd fallen in love with first. Then the rest of him in a rush.

Is it him, Twinkie? Is it my Dave?

"*I'm not sure,*" Twinkie said. "*Keep talking.*" She'd hidden behind the large stack of packages.

"What brings you in so late?" I asked him. Not that regular Dave would need a reason to come see me. I'd never asked him for a reason before.

"Maybe I just wanted to see you." He shrugged a shoulder. "Well, that and I was going to get some coffee. I'll be working late again tonight."

Working late wasn't an issue. Dave did that all the time. It was basically part of the job description.

Still, he'd usually run it by me first. As if I had a say, he'd ask if it was all right, and he'd ask if I was able to watch the girls, knowing full-well I was going to say yes to both questions.

Something was off, but maybe it wasn't as bad as I'd originally thought.

Like it had at the coffee counter, my face seemed to give everything away.

Dave grimaced. "Yeah, I know we haven't seen a lot of each other lately. And I'm sorry about that too. I'll, um, I'll make it up to you this weekend. Does that sound good? Let's have a date night."

"A date night?" I repeated.

"You know the place. Uh, Orange Blossoms or whatever. Does that work?"

"Sure."

Verdict?

"*Your head is in the way,*" Twinkie answered.

I tilted my head. "By the way, how *is* the investigation going? I'm guessing not so good... since you've got to work tonight... and you've worked a lot of others."

"Actually, it's okay." He brightened. "Mac's interviewing

some kid right now. We have a few solid leads. I'm tracking down something tonight. Something big. Or it could be."

"Care to share?" Real Dave would pucker at my brazen attempt to butt into the investigation.

He shook his head in a real Dave way. "For now, I'm keeping this one close to the chest. Plus, you aren't supposed to be worried about any of this."

"I'm not," I lied. "Although I wonder about this kid Mac's interviewing, if maybe he's a fan of *Creel Creek After Dark*?"

Dave squinted, as if he'd never heard of the podcast, then it clicked. "You know, I do recall seeing something about that in Mac's notes. Something about the chat messages in the last episode."

Dave said the words as if they meant nothing—as if he wasn't showing me his hand. Or rather, Mac's hand.

It's not him, I thought.

I knew.

A metallic voice sounded in my head. *Danger, Will Robinson, danger!*

At the same time, I had to do something about my face. I wrenched my lips up into a grin. "How about we get you that coffee?"

Dave looked hesitant, then finally nodded. "That sounds good."

The hits kept on coming. He didn't protest when I insisted on making him a latte in place of his usual drip. He even said he liked it.

I saw him out, then returned to the backroom for a debrief with Twinkie.

"It's not him," I told her, and she agreed. "Okay. Now that's settled. Why is he acting like this? Why is he trying to be Dave?"

"*Just a guess,*" Twinkie said. "*But I think he's fallen back to the reptilian side of the brain. Self-preservation—it's a funny thing. A snake survives with the threat of a bite and with venom. Humans use something equally toxic. They lie.*"

19

THE COLD CASEFILES OF SHERIFF MARSTERS AND MR. WOLF

OTHER DAVE

"She knows. I could see it in her eyes."

And?

"And she didn't say a word. Why?" In the rearview mirror, dark brown eyes glared back at me.

If I had to guess, Dave thought, *it's cause Constance will deal with this in her way.*

"How's that?"

I threw the SUV into motion, sending it careening backwards, but stopping it before it hit the dumpster in the gravel parking lot of Bewitched Books.

After a few days, I was getting the hang of it. It was *almost* natural. Like riding a bike—except I'd never done that either.

Instead, the phrase had bubbled up into my subconscious along with Dave's infernal thoughts.

Magic, he thought. *She turns to magic at times like this.*

"Not good," I said, glancing in the mirror before whipping the SUV into the street. It barreled over a curb. I over-corrected and sent it into the vacant other lane. Finally, I straightened it out and stepped on the gas.

Not good for you, maybe.

Considering it was magic that did the switcheroo on us, I thought it might be just as easy for it to swap us back.

I scoured Dave's mind for answers, but he seemed to have a limited knowledge of magic.

He knew about potions. The one he'd accidentally taken was called daylight. There wasn't a name for its counter, which we'd also taken. And according to his mind, there was no such thing as a counter to the counter-potion.

It wasn't the potion that did this to us, Dave thought. *At least I don't think so. Something else happened. Something else went wrong.*

"What about spells?" I asked.

What about them?

"If Constance finds a spell, it would, so to speak, spell trouble for me."

That is *the idea.*

Not good. I wasn't ready to give this up... not yet.

Maybe not ever.

I wasn't going to go down without a fight.

You said that wasn't a threat.

"It's a turn of phrase," I said. "I'm not going to fight her."

Then what are you going to do?

"The opposite," I said. "Besides. I like my chances. Did you see her back there at the store? She's as in control of her magic as you are of your body right now."

A jolt of stinging pain shot down my spine, nearly causing me to lose control of the vehicle.

"What was that?"

A warning. It's only a matter of time before I do get control.

"You nearly killed us."

I did not. You're going fifteen miles-per-hour... in a forty-five.

"I'm going with the speed of traffic."

You're in a cop car. They're afraid to pass you. Speed up. Where are you going, anyway? And what do you mean by the opposite? What's your plan with Constance?

"I'm chasing down a lead," I said, using some detective jargon found in the recesses of Dave's mind, in an old episode of *Law and Order*.

And you're not going to tell me what it is?

"I'll let you know if I need you."

And with Constance?

"I already told you. I'm not going to fight her. I'm going to do what you do. I'm going to love her."

I could feel Dave's protest bubbling to the surface. He wanted to sting me with pain again. So, I locked him in the recesses of my—and his—mind before he had the chance.

Right now, I had more pressing concerns than Constance reversing the spell.

The car rolled to a stop in the fire lane at Creel Creek Commons.

Inside, I bypassed the reception desk and retraced the steps to Maude Jenkins's room.

Her door was ajar.

The elderly woman was snoozing in her recliner. An episode of *The Andy Griffith Show* drowned out the sound of her snores.

It also drowned out the sound of me closing the door behind me.

And locking it.

Standing over her aged and frail body, I wrestled against an urge to snuff the life away from her.

It would be easy.

And quiet.

I allowed the urge to pass, then instead of throttling her, I cleared my throat. "Uh hum."

Maude blinked her eyes open. At first, her attention went back to the show. She startled when they finally found me in her view.

It wasn't startling enough to stop her heart. Not even enough to make her scream.

The *other* me though—he might have such an effect.

"Sheriff." Her voice sounded like a lifelong smoker, rattling and raspy. "What are you doing here in my room?"

"I was hoping to have a chat."

She reached for her water cup on the end table and took a long sip through its plastic straw, her eyes focused on me throughout it. It was unsettling.

The old bag was much more intimidating awake.

"Where's your lover?" she asked. "Don't you need her for chats? Or maybe you don't plan on being a lump today."

"No, not today," I said. "Today, I came prepared."

Her expression told me she wasn't convinced. She took another sip of water, waiting for me to start.

I eked out the words. "I have a few more questions in regard to your husband."

"Questions?" Maude scoffed. "Shouldn't you have answers by now, Sheriff? For instance, did you figure out what happened to him?"

"We haven't," I said. "Not definitively. The working theory is he might've fallen down a steep embankment or maybe been crushed in a mudslide. You see, several of his bones were broken, and there were some odd markings on his ribcage."

"What kind of markings?"

"Almost like he was scraped with something... something sharp."

"Scraped." She pretended to consider what it meant.

"Like maybe with a knife or another sharp object," I said.

"Like claws, maybe," she suggested.

"Possibly." I grinned inwardly.

I was almost positive Maude thought she was playing me—when, in fact, it was the other way around.

She'd said exactly what I'd hoped she would.

"Anyway, I have a few questions, if you don't mind."

"But I do mind, Sheriff. Why should I answer any of your questions when you can't answer the most basic thing of all—how was my husband killed? And was he murdered?"

"I already told you," I told her. "I can't answer that today. Not definitively."

"Maybe you should just come back when you can."

"Oh, I will," I said. "But first, I'm going to ask you these questions. They're simple enough, with what I assume will be simple answers."

"You know what happens when you assume, Sheriff."

The answer popped into Dave's mind. I chuckled as Maude's gray eyes studied me.

"The other day, when you met my friend Constance—"

"Your lover," Maude interjected.

"Right, that." Her words hit me harder than I wanted them to.

I wasn't bluffing with Dave in the car. My plan was simple. Love Constance and make Constance love me.

But she might never be my lover. She might never love me, not like with Dave.

And right now, she hated me. She didn't even know me. Not really.

She wasn't even willing to try.

After our short interaction at the bookstore, Constance was going to perform some spell to be rid of me.

If it worked, I'd go poof—back into Dave's subconscious.

Then I'd never get to see *this* through.

"Well," I continued. "Constance asked you if there was ever a tent or any gear recovered. You said no. I double checked."

"And?" Maude's cheeks puckered. "Did they ever find anything?"

"They didn't—which I thought was a little odd considering there was a search party. You know, they covered nearly twenty square miles, including the area where the body was eventually discovered."

"I don't see where you're going with this, Sheriff."

"Yeah, well, I wasn't sure either. But I had an instinct. You see, I sort of have a nose for things like this."

"Do you, now?" Maude's face contorted into what she thought to be a smile.

It was sinister.

"Yeah, so, I tracked someone down—it's something I'm good at. Does the name Elder Carmical ring any bells?"

"He another friend of yours?" she asked.

"No." I shook my head. "He worked with Frank at the insurance company. It's funny. The other day, I didn't realize the company that refused to pay out your benefit was the same company your husband had worked for for nearly three decades."

"They knew me," she spat. "They thought they could take advantage."

"Or." I shrugged my shoulders. "Perhaps, they suspected foul play?"

"What are you saying, Sheriff?"

I wasn't going to answer her directly. "Elder Carmical is

still alive and kicking. He plays a round of golf every Satur-day. He goes to church every Sunday. On Tuesdays, he volunteers to count the church offering. I caught up with him on Wednesday at the library, where he reads to chil-dren. We had a nice chat."

"I still don't see where this is going, Sheriff."

"Yeah, well, I'm new to delivering news like this."

Maude's eyes narrowed. Her mouth opened, then shut. It opened again. She was about to say something when the door shook violently.

On the other side, someone was trying to get in the room. They rapped on the door with quick knocks like a woodpecker on its favorite tree.

"Just a minute," I called, then I whispered so that only Maude could hear me, "Elder told me Franklin Jenkins never went on a hike in his life. He says Franklin used to complain about bugs when they sold insurance door to door."

Maude made a hacking sound to clear her throat, but she didn't say anything.

"Elder says there's no way Franklin went out that weekend to camp in the woods. He simply hoped that Franklin had left you for good. That's what the whole office wanted to believe. But days and then weeks and a year passed."

Another knock on the door. "Mrs. Franklin?" a female voice called. "Is everything all right in there?"

Neither of us answered.

Maude's throaty rasp sent a chill down my spine. "What do you think happened, Sheriff?"

She was so much more intimidating awake.

Still, I answered her. "I think the camping trip is a story you made up."

"And why would I do that?"

"Because you wanted them to find a body. In fact, I'd wager you were surprised when they didn't. But no big deal. It worked out for you... in the end."

"You don't know a lick," she said, then louder, "Emily, you can come in now. Use your key, if you have to."

A second later, the door was unlocked. A nurse stepped cautiously into the room.

"Why was the door locked?" she questioned as she closed it behind her. She wore teal scrub pants and a plain black t-shirt. That was also how I would describe her —plain.

The nurse didn't have many distinguishing features aside from a pair of cat-eye glasses. Her hair was brown and tied back into a neat ponytail.

Something about her presence lifted Maude's spirits. The old woman straightened.

"Emily, my girl." Maude began the process of letting the legs down on the recliner. "Have you met the sheriff?"

The nurse recoiled in surprise. "Sheriff?" she said. Then, regaining some composure, "Was it you who locked the door?"

"We were having a private conversation."

"Oh, well, I guess I could come back..."

"Not necessary," I said. "In fact, I was just leaving. Nice talking with you again, Maude. We'll catch up again soon, all right?"

"Soon?" she rasped. "Next time, Sheriff, I'll be prepared."

"Sounds good." I wasn't going to let an eighty-year-old woman get to me.

And yet, she's getting to you.

I didn't remember allowing Dave out of his box. He was

getting stronger. No telling how much longer I'd be able to keep him from invading more than his own mind.

"Shut up," I said, marching down the hallway.

So, that's what this was all about? You think Dad's innocent.

"You heard Maude. Was that the voice of an innocent woman?"

A nurse leaned out of an open doorway. It was Jennifer, the same girl from the first visit. "Is everything okay, Sheriff?"

You've really got to stop talking to yourself, Dave thought.

"Will you shut up until we get to the car?" I muttered under my breath.

The nurse's eyebrows shot up quizzically.

"Fine," I told her. "Everything's just fine."

"It doesn't sound fine." She smiled. "What about Maude? Is everything okay with her? You know, she got a little worked up during your last visit. I didn't want to say anything at the time, but her blood pressure was high. I should probably go check on her now."

"Not necessary," I said. "What's her name, Emily, is in there with her."

"She would be," Jennifer said sourly.

It was my turn to raise an eyebrow.

"Oh, those two are as thick as thieves. If you ask me, Emily gets a little too close to the patients."

I wasn't asking her, but the notion was intriguing. What all had Maude shared with her pal Emily? Perhaps she knew of Maude's dark deeds.

"Is that right?"

I hoped for more intrigue but only found gossip. "I think maybe she's just lonely. She's been in a long-term, long-distance relationship for a while now. You know how it goes."

I didn't, but I pretended I did. "I think Maude might've mentioned something about him. Called him Emily's lover."

"Lover? Really?" Jennifer laughed. "It's funny, I don't actually know if they've ever met."

"You said they were in a relationship?"

"Online." She lowered her voice. "A few of us thought she might be getting catfished."

I had to rack Dave's brain for the meaning. "Huh."

"Sorry." Jennifer smiled. "I'm giving you way more info than you bargained for. I'll shut up now. But if you need anything else, Sheriff, just let me know."

I thanked her and didn't make another stop until we reached the car.

We—as in the royal we. Me, myself, and Other Dave.

I hate to say it, but you might be right... about Maude... about Dad...

"Might be?" I adjusted the rearview mirror and bore a hole into our eyes. "Dave, you see what this means, right? It was a setup. Dad never recovered from this. It's why he ran away."

He's not the only reason he ran.

"You just hate it," I told him. "You hate that I'm right."

It's not that. I just don't know why it matters. What does proving his innocence do for you? For us?

"I don't know," I answered honestly.

But it felt important—like something I had to do.

The thing was, I didn't think I could do it alone.

I needed some help.

And thanks to Dave's thoughts, I knew exactly where to find it.

20

MOONLIT MAGIC

A t its best, magic is as easy as wishing something—anything—into existence.

It's exactly what I dreamed magic would be as a kid.

Take what happened with the hovering chair in the storeroom of Bewitched Books. I didn't need to make up a rhyme. Nor did I have to will my magic from the depths of the shadow realm.

It just worked.

But that was not how my magic always liked to manifest.

In fact, it was hardly ever so easy.

Magic had proven to be a fickle friend of mine. Sometimes, it worked like a charm, so to speak, but more often than not, it failed in some way or another.

There was, however, a silver lining. There were ways to manipulate the outcome—several steps a witch could take to increase her chances of magical success.

The problem was I didn't have the time or patience for many of those odds enhancing endeavors.

I wanted results sooner, rather than later.

I needed Dave back now.

Who knew what the *other* him might be up to now. And how he might mess up the investigation.

Or worse—get Dave locked away for a crime he hadn't committed.

So, I wasn't waiting for a crescent moon to appear in the sky. Overhead, the moon hung half-full.

I wanted to curse at it but grumbled instead.

The time glowed on my smart watch, reminding me it was nowhere near the witching hour but instead a half-hour after dusk.

I had to get back to the girls soon.

Mom was covering for me... again.

But I would be able to enhance the spell using the grave-yard and the old oak tree inside it.

I parked outside Gran's house. I hadn't set a foot inside it, not in a long while. It made me uncomfortable. I missed her, and going back there made it worse.

There were so many things left unsaid between us—not to mention between her and Mom.

Skirting around the back fence, I found the worn path through the woods.

Tonight, I wasn't expecting others. No Trish or Kalene. No Lauren. They'd be here at the next crescent moon but not sooner. So, when I saw a shadow looming in the path ahead, I stopped in my tracks.

Not a single chill ran down my spine, allowing me to breathe easier. My witchy senses claimed no danger lay ahead.

Shadows are funny things. Depending on the lighting, they can either squash or elongate the person who casts them. In this case, neither was true. The shadow's outline was of a man, but it wasn't a man hunched ahead on the path. A raccoon waved to me. He stood in the middle of the path where it opened to the clearing and the graveyard at its center.

"Brad?"

"*You didn't want to bring the whole coven?*"

"We're not a coven," I said. "And no. This is my mess-up. I'll deal with it myself. Plus, they're all so busy with their love lives."

"*You used to have one of those.*"

"I still do," I said. "Or I will, once this gets settled."

Brad clambered through the dead grass and leaves up the sloping hill.

He stopped at the rusty iron gates of the graveyard. Both hung limp on their frames. The fence was equally mangled and worn. Parts of it had caved in on itself, and yet somehow, it still managed to hold a barrier to the outside world.

"*This spell you want to do tonight,*" Brad said. "*I'm not sure it's wise to try it alone. Not without at least another witch as backup.*"

"Then I guess I won't be wise tonight."

"*Constance, you understand I have your best interests in mind. Don't you?*"

"What does it matter?" I asked him. "If it works, it works. If not, I'll try again another time. And another."

"*You know what they say about doing something over and over again and expecting a different result.*"

"They call it practice?" I shrugged. "What do you expect me to do? Leave Dave stuck in there somewhere while this *other* guy takes over the show?"

"*You could wait for the full moon,*" Brad suggested.

"You think that will reverse it?"

He shrugged, his raccoon paws going well above his shoulders. "*It might.*"

"That's weeks away," I said. "There're two crescent moons before that happens."

"*So try then.*"

"Brad... what's this trepidation about? Be honest."

"*The Moon.*" He gazed up at it. "*She's as finicky as magic, and she's more temperamental than Mother Gaia.*"

"Wait... are you saying the moon—"

"*She's a goddess, yes.*"

"You never told me that before?"

"*I didn't think I'd have to spell it out for you.*"

I sighed. "From now on, maybe just spell everything out."

His eyes glowed in the darkness. "*Listen. Your connection with her isn't like it is with the Mother. It's not like the connection Dave has with the Moon either.*"

"But we are connected... somehow?"

He nodded solemnly. "*She and Mother Gaia are sisters. When you go to the tree, you'll be asking a lot of Mother Gaia— asking her to speak to her sister, a sister she hasn't spoken to in, well, in a long, long time.*"

"Okay..."

"*Do you see now why I don't want you trying this spell over and over again?*"

"I get it. You don't want me coming off like a bratty two-year-old."

"*Something like that,*" Brad agreed.

"I guess it's a good thing we kind of have an in with Mother Gaia."

He shook his head. "*I know it's been a while since you last talked to her, but you do remember how your grandmother can be? Her status with the Mother isn't something she'll surrender for you or for anyone. If she thinks this is a bad idea, she'll be the first to talk Mother Gaia out of it.*"

"Good point," I said. Then I strode through the gate and up the hill where Brad wouldn't follow.

Witch customs declared familiars weren't welcome on the sacred ground of the graveyard.

But that didn't stop his words from lingering in my head.

When I'd started here, I wanted a simple spell. I wanted easy magic. This was as opposite from easy as it gets.

It was one thing for a spell to need the approval of Mother Gaia—for her to allow the magic to pass through the shadow realm to the earth.

This was a whole other ballgame.

Although, I'd asked the Mother for favors in the past, and she'd granted every last one.

I couldn't help but wonder if I'd redeemed my last token.

Was she going to say no?

Even if she said yes, what would her sister say?

Had the Moon orchestrated this?

It shone brightly on the hill, eerily illuminating the gravestones, which poked up crookedly on the side of the hill.

Dead leaves crunched beneath my feet. A tuft of moss stuck to the bottom of my shoe. I kicked it away as I reached my hand out to the old oak tree.

As always, it accepted my magic which glowed with a blue energy—the same color as my eyes.

The magic sparkled around my fingertips and fizzled into the trunk.

"Mother Gaia, hear my plea.
Bring my lover back to me.
If it's the Moon that did him wrong,
Can you speak to her? I know it's been long.
I'll do anything you ask. That I swear.

Anything, just please hear out my prayer."

"Mother Gaia," I whispered, breaking the rhyme I hadn't thought out. "Please do something. Anything to help me get Dave back."

A branch snapped above me, and this time, a chill did run down my spine. But my magic was spent, all of it cast into the tree with the spell.

I looked up and found an owl perched high on a limb. Its lantern-like eyes gazed down at me.

It hooted.

Owls always reminded me of my mother.

But this was just an owl. It stretched out its wings, then flew away.

Captivated, I watched it disappear into the inky black sky.

I barely registered the shadow that crossed between myself and the moon above. The hairs on my neck stood on end.

I turned to find a man standing between me and the gates below.

"You want your Dave back, huh." He smiled, but it was unrecognizable. I'd never seen those lips stretched so thin and so crooked.

"Dave?"

He shook his head.

Dave's head.

"Afraid I'm not," he said. "But you already knew that."

21

OTHER DAVE AND THE TREE OF TRUST

OTHER DAVE

Constance tensed, as if I were a threat. In her mind, I probably was.

Me—the anti-Dave. Everything she loved about him, she hated about me in equal measure.

I wondered how I could change her mind.

You can't, Dave thought.

But I knew he was wrong.

Taking a step back, I gave Constance space and a path down the hill, if she chose to take it.

Then I cleared my throat. "What I meant to say is I knew at the bookstore that you'd figured it out."

"Figured what out, exactly?"

"I can't read your mind," I said. "I'm not like you're familiar. But I know that you know I'm not really Dave."

She inched away, choosing the path I'd given her.

I was scaring her, and for probably the first time in my existence, I was hoping to do the opposite.

Constance shut her eyes tightly, collecting her thoughts.

"Except I still don't really know what it all means. If you're not Dave, then who are you? The wolf?"

"No," I said. "And yes."

"Well, which is it?"

"It's complicated." Except it wasn't really. "Technically I *am* Dave. But another version."

A better version.

Now you learn the art of internal thought? Dave questioned. *You are not a* better *version.*

Constance's eyes were so blue in the moonlight. They were glassy and perfect. She was truly stunning.

"How?" she asked.

"How what?" I asked.

"How is it that I'm talking to you and not him? Was it the potions?"

I shook my head. "I'm not sure. Your guess is as good as mine. Probably better. The truth is, we don't know how it happened. We just woke up like this."

"We?"

"He's in here too," I told her. "Somewhere."

I'm right here, Constance, Dave reassured.

"When—when did you wake up like this?"

"The day after that big headache."

No surprise registered on her face, but she blinked a beat too long. "So, you've been lying to me since then."

"Lying?" I didn't understand her meaning.

"Acting like you're him when you're obviously not."

"What was I supposed to do?" I asked. "I don't even know you. Or I didn't at the time. I woke up and the world was... different."

"You still don't know me," she said. "But you could've told me what was happening. I would've tried to help you."

"You would've tried to put me back in the box."

"What box?" Her glassy eyes were searching for under-standing. "What are you talking about?"

"Dave—he locks me up in here." I pressed a finger to my temple. "We don't cross paths, not anymore. We don't talk. I woke up in a world I didn't recognize, a world I'd only had brief glimpses of... because of him."

There was no use telling her about the other time he'd let me out. Not now.

Constance had stopped inching down the hill. She was stooped sideways, her left leg higher on the hill than the right.

"You're scaring me," she said.

"I don't want to scare you, Constance."

Except my words had stirred a panic. Again, she began to back away. This time, she slipped on a pile of leaves.

My reflexes were as quick as they ever were. I lunged after her, catching her before she could fall and bust her skull on a headstone.

We stayed rooted in that spot a moment.

Constance in my arms.

She was so warm. Her heart beat fast and hard. I felt it in my own chest.

"Then what do you want?"

"I want—"

I want you, I thought.

Don't say that, Dave's voice sounded in my head.

He was right. Telling her this truth wasn't the right thing to do.

"—I want your help."

Her eyes were questioning and unsure. She recoiled, as if I'd said my truth. Pushing me away, she stood up straight and dusted herself off.

"You followed me here," she said.

"No," I said. "I waited here thirty minutes for you to show up."

She coughed out a laugh. "You know that's worse, right?"

It did sound bad.

"I don't get it," she said. "You came up here. You waited for me. And you didn't stop the spell?"

"No," I said.

"Why not?"

I shrugged. "Because I didn't think it would work."

She scrubbed her face. "Why not? Do you know something I don't?"

"No," I answered honestly. "It just feels like I'm meant to be here. I'm here for a reason."

"And that is?"

"To reunite Dave and our father."

It wasn't the answer she expected. "And you want my help with that?"

"And with the case." I nodded.

No, Dave thought. *You promised.*

I'm altering the deal, I thought, and the words brought up a memory of a dark figure dressed in black.

She looked unsure. "And if I don't—if I don't help you— if I wait for the full moon to take you away. What then?"

I shrugged again. "If that's what you think it'll do. It's funny though. He doesn't want you to help me either. But you're probably the only person who can."

"That sounds like him." She smiled. "How do I know I can trust you?"

"You don't have to trust me, Constance." Although I wanted her to—I wanted her to more than anything.

She's still trying to get rid of you, Dave reminded me.

"If you help me," I said. "I'll let him out."

"Meaning?" She narrowed her eyes.

"Meaning I'll let you speak to Dave."

"But I won't trust you," she said.

The wind blew through the branches of the oak tree above us. At first, I thought leaves were falling. Then I noticed the tree's branches were bare.

Blue sparkles of dust rained down upon us, sprinkling our shoulders. I twisted the stuff between my fingers. "What is this?"

"Magic," Constance said. "It's my magic."

"What's it doing?"

Momentarily, I was afraid—afraid her spell had finally taken effect, and I was about to be switched out with the real Dave.

"I *think* it wants me to trust you."

"Why would it want that?" I asked.

She brushed her thumb and forefinger together, flinging magical blue dust into the air. "Why indeed."

22

SUMMER SHIELDS AND THE FANBOY

With her eyes locked on the entrance, Summer Shields absentmindedly drummed chipped fingernails against the table.

Rap a tap tap.

Rap a tap tap.

The sound reverberated around the cafe. Bewitched Books was as dead as it used to be back when it was only a used bookstore—long before the renovations and before we began serving coffee.

A single customer roved the bookshelves.

In Creel Creek, being associated with a murder was its own sort of death sentence.

But it was also like a rite of passage. Almost every store —every commercial venture from the local hotel to the vineyard and the grocery store—everyone had experienced something like this.

I knew in time the stigma would pass. We just had to stick it out until it did.

For now, the lack of bustle was a good thing. It gave me time to think. And to help Summer.

We sat at a table at the edge of the cafe, waiting for someone. Summer wouldn't tell me who, but I knew this had something to do with the murder investigation—the same investigation Other Dave wanted my help with.

Summer inspected her nails. "I should go get a manicure. Shouldn't I?"

She waved her chipped nails in my direction.

"I guess so." I clenched my hands, so she wouldn't see mine were worse.

"No, really, I should. I have a big date on Friday."

"Yeah? Where to?" I didn't feel at all jealous that Trish and Summer's dating lives were booming while mine went to, for lack of better words, hell.

Although it could be worse. At least I wasn't dating a demon, just the other side of the man I truly loved.

"It's nothing fancy," Summer said. "Carver's taking me to Orange Blossoms. It's our one-month anniversary."

"Is that still a thing?"

"Anniversaries?" Summer raised a thin eyebrow. "Uh, yeah, anniversaries are still a thing. Don't tell me you and Dave no longer celebrate."

"Then I won't tell you," I said.

"Constance!"

"No, we do celebrate." I hesitated, trying to remember the last one.

Dave had taken me on a vacation we'd both very much needed, to commemorate another year had passed. We were well past the monthly or every six month phase.

This wasn't high school after all.

"We celebrate the big ones," I said. "It's just when you've been dating for—"

"A while now," she interjected. "I get it. I do. But sweetie, you're not married to the man. You can't let the years go by without—" She tried to find the words. "—without him putting in some effort."

"He does put in effort," I argued halfheartedly. "Or he did. I mean he does when he's not... well... like he is now."

Summer's thin eyebrows shot up in question. "How is he, this *other* guy?"

"In what way?"

"In every way." She smiled, and I knew where this was going.

"He's different," I said.

"I know he's different. But he's kind of the same, isn't he? It all sounds kinda sexy to me."

"Well, he's not sexy."

Except he looked a whole lot like Dave on the outside, and his voice had a growl to it, which was totally *not* sexy except for when it was.

"Come on, Constance. You know I can tell you like him."

"He's Dave," I said. "I mean sort of. Of course I like him."

"They're the same guy." She shrugged. "Why not let yourself like him? Why not give him a go, if you know what I mean."

Luckily, I wasn't drinking my coffee. If I had been, I would've snorted it out.

"Oh, I know what you mean," I said. "But they're not really the same guy. In fact, I made other him sleep on the couch last night. And I still wasn't comfortable. Maybe I should send him packing. He can sleep at Gran's."

"You're joking."

"I'm not," I said. "You know, it's kinda funny. He was trying to get me to go on a date with him the other day. This was before I knew. Obviously, I can't go now."

"Why not?" Summer laughed. "Oh, you totally should! Go out with him. Dave's not going to mind you eating a meal with the man. Plus, we can meet up and you can meet Carver. I'd love to know what you think of him."

"I'm not sure that's a good idea."

"Oh, you'll love Carver."

"That's not what I meant. I'm sure I'll like your boyfriend. It's mine who's the problem."

"You're making him a problem," she said. "You haven't even given him a chance."

"You talk like him."

"Then he makes a good point." She smirked. "And I think Carver would like a double date. He's new in town and hasn't met many people yet."

"He met you," I said. "Y'all met at that speed dating thing, right?"

"Right." She nodded, then narrowed her eyes. "Who told you? That was supposed to be a secret outing."

"Trish," I said. "And it's hard to keep a secret when all of you met someone there."

"Figures." Summer shook her head. "Trish only keeps your secrets. Well, that and her own. I wish I'd caught a glimpse of her new sweetheart, but I don't think I did. Or if I did, I don't remember. And no, I didn't see Lauren or Kalene's either. That's kinda funny, right?"

"It is," I agreed.

Summer checked her phone. "This guy better be dead."

Shaking my head, I got up to warm our coffees. "Don't say that. The way things tend to go in this town, he might be. When was he supposed to be here?"

"Twenty minutes ago." Summer sighed and tapped out a text message.

"Maybe he got held up." I slid her coffee across the table.

"Or" —she eyed the customer browsing the shelves— "he's been here the whole time."

The young man pulled his phone from his pocket.

"I knew it," Summer said, then she called over to him, "Come on, kid. I don't have all day."

The guy was in his early to mid-twenties. He was medium height and wiry. Shaggy blond curls spilled out of a beanie on top of his head.

Hesitantly, he made his way over to us. "Athena Hunter, it's an honor to finally make your acquaintance."

"It would've been an honor twenty minutes ago, too," Summer shot back.

"Sorry." He stared at his own worn out shoes. "I was trying to work up the nerve. I, uh, I've never met a celebrity before."

"I'm not a celebrity. Not really."

"You are though." He brightened. "You're on the podcast. You're one of the stars of ParaTube. Not to mention the news. You're on TV every day."

"Five days a week," she said. "It's a local affiliate. It's nothing. We don't even reach Charlottesville."

"Like that matters!" He scoffed. "The broadcast signal might not be strong, but it's all online these days anyway."

"Yeah, it's on our website," she agreed. "Which gets a few hundred hits a day. It's peanuts."

"No," he disagreed. "Once someone figured out Athena Hunter and Summer Shields were one and the same, we started uploading your news stories to our fan site. You get millions of hits a day."

"I do?" Summer cringed in my direction. "Wait. There's a fan site?"

"Several." He pulled on the chair beside Summer. "Mind if I sit?"

"Go ahead." Summer sipped her coffee. "You're the whole reason we're here."

Not technically true. I was supposed to be working. But he was the reason she was here.

He sat down, and Summer made introductions. "Constance, this is Evan. Evan, this is Constance. She's a part owner here and sometimes a topic on the show—although we've never used her real name."

"Oh!" Evan's eyes widened. For a second, I thought he wanted to say something—maybe to apologize for the shenanigans in the store last week—but instead, his mouth opened, and it continued to gush over Summer.

This was what he was holding back for twenty minutes —his love and adoration for the *Creel Creek After Dark* podcast and his favorite host, Athena Hunter.

I couldn't blame him there. Of the two hosts, Summer was the more palatable.

Jade was an acquired taste, although she'd mellowed out since her run-in with Morgana—a familiar Ivan had conspired with, giving her control of Jade's mind and body for months while Jade's soul was trapped in the body of a cardinal.

Evan gushed for a while longer, and Summer raked it in. Half my coffee refill was gone before she finally steered the conversation over to the topic at hand. "Evan," she said, "while it's always nice to hear from our fans, there was a reason I reached out to you. There are a few things I wanted to clear up. Things like what were you and those other fans doing in here last week?"

Evan went pale. "You... you know I already talked to the police, right?"

Summer smiled in a way that said she'd heard comments like this a thousand times or more. "We understand completely if it feels like you're having to answer the same questions over and over again. The thing is our local law enforcement doesn't like to give us journalists much to go on. They like to pretend it's because we get in their way. But we all know the truth—they're afraid we'll solve the case before they do."

"Yeah, but the detective—he encouraged me not to talk with the media."

"I'm not asking about the murder," Summer said. "I'm asking what you were doing in a bookstore."

"Right." Evan nodded. "And he did say it was ultimately my decision if I wanted to talk to anybody else, so..."

"So, what's your decision, Evan?" Summer asked. "Are you willing to talk to us?"

"I guess so." He shrugged. "I don't think it's going to hurt anything."

"Why do you say that?" I asked him.

He shrugged again. "The same reason I didn't ask for a lawyer yesterday. I don't know anything much."

"I'll be the decider of that," Summer said. "Let's start here. This *is* where it started, right? You were here with some other fans?"

"I guess." His eyes wandered toward the glamoured section of spell books and witching supplies. "But what we did here wasn't a crime, if that's what you're saying."

"My co-owner thinks you were trespassing," I told him.

"Not true!" he shot back. "There's not a sign back there or anything. We didn't know we weren't supposed to be back there."

"Is that true?" Summer asked him. "You *really* didn't know? Because I'll tell you what, Evan. I'm good at catching people in lies. It's sort of what I do for a living. And that sounded like a lie to me."

I wanted to know how someone without a drop of

magical blood could know anything was back there besides a section of books in their most hated subject.

Evan frowned. "Okay. I was lying. We knew something was back there."

"How?" I asked.

He looked to Summer, as if she might bail him out. When she didn't, he sighed and carried on. "We came here just to check it out. It's been talked about on the podcast a few times. I think we all spotted those grimoires over there as fakes. So, we started comparing notes. We all saw a different section over there."

Now I knew we needed to try a new glamour.

"And how did you know Tyson Briggs?" Summer's question didn't catch him as off-guard as it caught me.

"That's kind of the thing," he said. "I didn't. Not really."

Summer narrowed her eyes. "Wasn't Tyson with you? That's about the only thing Detective Mackenzie was willing to tell me."

"It's true," Evan agreed. "I *did* meet Tyson here. Like meet meet. It was the first time we met in person. Any of us."

"How many of you were there?" I asked.

"A few." He counted on his fingers. "Five, counting me. The funny thing is, I didn't know Tyson's real name. We all used our handles when we met here."

"What kind of handles?" Summer asked. "Are you gamers?"

"No." He flinched. "Well, yes. But this wasn't about a game. It was all about *Creel Creek After Dark*."

I hated that Mac looked to be right about a few things.

"We met on ParaTube," Evan said. "In the comments section. A group of us were always in the chat. Every episode. I started to see the same names, over and over. We grew a rapport. After a while, I set up a server for us to chat even when the show wasn't live.

"Uh huh." Summer took down notes.

"Since they haven't been airing lately, we were chatting more in my server space. Someone, I don't remember who, started talking about putting our own show together. Our own podcast. I thought we should meet first. We decided here would be the best place."

"Are the others local to Creel Creek?" I asked him.

He shook his head. "I think a few of them live within a couple of hours of here. I mean, no one balked at making the trip, if that's what you're asking."

It wasn't. "What about you? Do you live here in town?"

He shook his head again. "Nah, I'm in college over in Lynchburg."

"So you're not too far away," I said. "Have you ever come here to explore on your own?"

"A few times," he said, his eyes lingering over the section he couldn't see. "I camped outside the city once. I like camping. I waited for the fog to roll in the next morning, and it did—just like the podcast said it would."

Camping. It reminded me of Maude's husband. The *other* body we'd found.

"What about the others?" Summer asked.

"Like I said before, I don't really know them."

"Except online." Summer made a face only her notebook could see. When she lifted her chin, her features had straightened. "Why don't you tell us about Tyson. What was he like?"

"He seemed all right at first."

"What's that supposed to mean?" Summer locked eyes with me, as if she thought we might finally learn something.

I wasn't convinced.

Evan huffed. "I mean he wasn't confrontational—no matter what that detective wants to think. Tyson was a naysayer, yeah. But it wasn't like we were fighting with him."

"Naysayer?" Summer's pen came to an abrupt halt. "I'm not sure I'm following."

Evan pulled off his beanie and ran a hand through his blond locks. "I don't even know why Tyson came. Online, he went by Arwen Wolf, and he made out like he was really one of us. In fact, I think he's the one who suggested we do something on our own. But last week, he..."

"He what?" Summer pressed.

"He acted like it was a joke—like we were jokes. Or at least he said as much. He said he thought we were joking."

Now, I wasn't following. "Evan, what exactly did Tyson think you were joking about?"

"About the wolves," he said. "The werewolves, I mean. Or werewolf, depending on who you talk to."

My heart began to race.

"So, your little group"— Summer frowned — "it's about werewolves?"

"I know how it sounds. But I thought of anyone, you might understand."

"I'm just trying to get a clear picture of what you were here for." Summer's voice was calming. "It sounds like you came here to talk with some like-minded friends and maybe Tyson ruined it."

"Something like that," he said.

My mind was focused elsewhere. "So, you think you saw a werewolf?"

Evan's frustration with me was evident on his brow. "Everyone thinks I'm making it up. But I saw one. I swear. You asked if I'd ever been here before. I lied. I've been here lots of times. Out camping in the mountains."

"And that's where you think you saw this—this were-wolf?" Summer asked.

"I know I did," Evan said. "Honestly, that detective didn't think it was as funny as I thought he might. He asked *a lot* of questions."

I bet he did.

"Y'all don't believe me either."

"Is that what you think?" Summer asked. "I know I'm the more skeptical host, but in all my years living here, I've never put blinders on. Strange things happen in Creel Creek."

"What about you?" His gaze shifted heavily on me.

"I'm one of the witches they like to talk about."

He smirked at that. "Okay. So, you may not believe me, but at least you're listening. Tyson wouldn't listen."

"Meaning?" Summer asked.

"Meaning he talked a big game online—like he wanted us to go out and gather proof. Like he wanted to film it. But when we met, he said he was never serious about any of it."

"How did the others react?" We hadn't even discussed the other fans involved. In my mind, the other suspects.

"They weren't happy," Evan said. "We asked him to leave."

"And did he?"

"Not before making a scene. He's the one who ran over there to the restricted section and started throwing things around."

"Oh." Summer's jaw clenched.

"We all had to leave after that. And I know what you're going to ask. But that's it. I didn't see him again after that. As far as I know, no one did."

"Can I ask who the others were?" Summer's pen hovered over her notepad.

"I don't know their names," he said again. "But they're all in your last episode's chat. I can give you all of our handles."

"That would be great," Summer said. "What's your handle in the chat?"

"Cesaire," Evan said. "Not many people remember, but he's the wolf—"

"In the *Red Riding Hood* movie," Summer finished.

"Yeah." Evan beamed, his faith in his favorite podcaster renewed.

I was equally surprised with Summer's monster movie trivia knowledge. It showed in my open-mouthed stare.

"What?" She blanched. "I know my Billy Burke movies."

I racked my brain, putting a face with the name. "Isn't he the dad from *Twilight*?"

"Don't mock me when the guy you're dating looks like his evil twin brother."

Considering that Dave currently *was* his evil twin, that was about the worst thing Summer could've said. I went pink.

"Sorry." She winced. "Anyway, that's an interesting handle. Let me write down the others."

"They're all wolf themed. That's what drew us together in the first place." Evan rattled them off.

"I see." Summer's pen scribbled.

"Do you, maybe, want to meet them?" Evan lifted his chin, a hopeful gleam in his eyes. "Maybe we could talk about everything on the podcast?"

"As in you'd like to be a guest?"

"Not just me." Evan talked fast. "I mean we don't have to, but it could be cool, right? Cool's not the right word. But you know what I mean. I think the others would like it. They really wanted to start this podcast, and Tyson kind of, well, he ruined everything."

"How dare he go out and die." I regretted the words as soon as they came out of my mouth.

I knew Evan didn't mean to be so insensitive.

"I meant before." He dropped his gaze to the table. "You're right though. It's a stupid idea."

"It's not." Summer put a soothing hand atop his. "Let me talk to Ivana, and we'll be in touch. We haven't had a guest on the show in ages. A big group of werewolf enthusiasts. That sounds... fun."

23

CREEL CREEK AFTER DARK

SEASON 3: EPISODE 13

It's getting late.
So very late.
You hear something go bump in the night.
Are you afraid?
You should be!
Welcome to Creel Creek After Dark.

Athena: I'm your host Athena Hunter.

Ivana: And I'm Ivana Steak.

Athena: Tonight, we have a spectacular show lined up for you. In fact, some listeners might recognize a few of our guests. But not by their faces or even their real names.

Ivana: What Athena is trying to say is you may recognize their handles.

Athena: Yes. Their screen names should be familiar if you've ever popped into the ParaTube chat because our guests today are fans of the show, just like you.

Ivana: For over a year, they've been livening up the chat with colorful commentary.

Athena: Not too colorful!

Ivana: No. Not *too* colorful. And it's important to note, they'll only be using their screen names tonight. Not only will it make it less confusing for you listeners, but it will also protect their anonymity.

Athena: Kind of like a pseudonym. Funny. I have one of those too.

Ivana: As do I, Athena. But let's bring it back around to our guests. I believe you said they're fans of the show?

Athena: And that's not the only thing they have in common...

Ivana: You have me in suspense.

Athena: All five of our guests today have had close encounters of the wolf-ish kind.

Ivana: By that, you mean they've seen a werewolf and lived to tell the tale?

Athena: So they say, Ivana. But you know me—I'm a little skeptical when somebody cries wolf.

Ivana: As we all should be, Athena. But it's important we allow them to have their say, and as always, we want our listeners and our viewers on ParaTube to make up their own minds.

Athena: Let's welcome The Hidden Werewolf Society to the show. With us tonight, we have Cesaire, Ginger Snaps, New Moon, Remus, and Chewbarka—I'm guessing you're a bit of a *Star Wars* fan?

Chewbarka (Yoda voice): Seen it several times, I have.

Athena: **chuckles**

Ivana: And Remus, is that of the Lupin variety?

Remus: Too right. Best Defense Against the Dark Arts teacher Hogwarts ever had.

Athena: I think we can all agree on that.

Ivana: Cesaire, Ginger, New Moon... welcome to the show.

Cesaire: Thanks. Happy to be here.

New Moon: Long time listener. First time caller.

Ivana: New Moon, I get the Twilight reference. But Ginger, I'm afraid with your handle, I'm a tad lost.

Ginger Snaps: Oh, it's an indie flick from the early 2000s. It's hard to find werewolf movies from the female perspective.

New Moon: She speaks the truth. I almost went with Leah Clearwater but wasn't sure anyone would get the reference.

Athena: I would've.

Ivana: You get every movie reference, Athena.

Athena: It's one of my few skills, along with the ability to go three whole minutes without blinking.

Ivana: Now, now—let's not get *too* off track. We have this group here today for a couple of reasons. The first is they claim to have had run-ins with werewolves. The second is—

Ginger Snaps: Y'all promised not to bring him up.

Ivana: The second is their love and admiration for our show.

Ginger Snaps: Oh...

Athena: It's all right, Ginger. Although the audience might be wondering who exactly you mean.

Ginger Snaps: Can you cut that part out?

Athena: We could cut it from the podcast, sure. But we're live on ParaTube with nine thousand viewers tuning in. Make that ten.

Cesaire: Might as well tell them, Ginger. We know how the fandom can be. They're going to figure it out eventually, along with our real names, our occupations, and everything else.

Ivana: Figure what out? See, I'm as confused as a listener. Athena—what did you fail to mention to me before the show?

Athena: I didn't tell you that there used to be a sixth member to this werewolf gang. He went by the screen name Arwen Wolf, and…

Ivana: And what?

Athena: He was the young man killed in the woods last week.

Ivana: You mean the man who was killed by a werewolf?

Cesaire: That's not exactly where the evidence points.

Ginger Snaps: How would you know?

Cesaire: Because unlike you four, I was brought in for questioning.

Chewbarka: I was too.

Remus: Same here.

Athena: What about you two?

Ivana: Athena!

Athena: It's just a question.

Ivana: One we'll leave unanswered for now. Let's take a short break to highlight tonight's sponsors. And when we're back, let's hear more about these werewolf encounters.

[Dead Air]

24

THE HIDDEN WEREWOLF SOCIETY

C reel Creek After Dark was recorded in a small studio space on the upper floor of the Creel Creek Brewery.

They waited until well after midnight—well after my bedtime—to start the show. They claimed it was for the benefit of their fans. I knew better. They wanted the downstairs cleared of patrons, so there was quiet on the set.

Summer had me wait outside the recording booth for the show to start while she and Jade worked with their producer Simon to set up the microphones and other equipment.

There was a couch to lounge on, along with a coffee table. The spare chairs had to be moved inside the booth to fit all five members of the werewolf crew in with them.

To the outside world—or outside of the paranormal world—The Hidden Werewolf Society would sound a lot like conspiracy theorists prattling on about the differences between the werewolves of film and television and the real thing.

To most of the listeners, they'd sound crazy. Their ideas

wouldn't marry up to what the rest of the world thought of werewolves.

At least that was my hope.

The funny thing about conspiracy theorists is most look a whole lot like ordinary people. The same was true for this group.

Of the five, there were three men. A teenager went by the handle Chewbarka. During the taping, he kept his hood over his head, hiding a mane of long black hair.

A middle-aged man, without much hair, introduced himself to me as Frank. On the podcast, he went by Remus.

Then there was Evan, who was quiet but nodded to me when he walked in. During the first bit of the episode, he allowed Chewbarka and Remus to ham it up and hog the limelight.

Two women made up the rest of their group. They were either in their late twenties or early thirties. Both brunettes. They wore glasses of opposite styles—one cat eyed and stylish, the other plain and square.

Neither had introduced themselves to me before the show. But why would they? I wasn't a faux celebrity like Athena or Ivana.

These two were who interested me most.

Ginger Snaps in particular. She clammed up after she thought Jade might mention Tyson Briggs.

They took a long commercial break before finally restarting the episode.

Looks are one thing. Eventually, a conspiracy theorist has to speak, and the words that spill from their mouth, well, they catch people off-guard.

Their words caught me off-guard. Their ideas held merit. They each had a story to tell—a reason they believed.

Like Evan's story, Ginger's held my attention. It was

oddly reminiscent of a night when I was a fledging witch—
the night Dave was shot with a sterling silver bullet.

Ginger claimed to have been interning at the local
hospital when a man came in with a gunshot wound. He
was rushed through the emergency room and into surgery,
where he began shifting from one form to another. From a
man to a beast and vice-versa. All the while, the doctor
removed the jinxed metal from his flesh.

The story gave me chills, and it wasn't only because it
was a story I knew. My magic was sending me a warning
about Ginger.

Had she killed Tyson Briggs? And if she did, why?

New Moon's story sounded like a piece of *Twilight* fanfic-
tion. Except the love story was believable.

She had dated a man who disappeared around the time
of the full moon. He ghosted her calls and texts, then he'd
return the next morning dog-tired, as if he'd fully exerted
himself the night before.

The story didn't hold as many details as Ginger's. This
was another thing I'd lived through. When Dave came home
the morning after a full moon, he was dark eyed with twigs
in his hair. He'd crash and be hard to wake up until the next
morning, his body spent from the shift into wolf form and
the miles spent chasing deer around a mountain.

New Moon's ex sounded more like a lying, cheating
bastard. I'd known a few of those in my life.

For good measure, I sent a silent curse at my ex-husband
Mark—one of many I'd gifted him since becoming a witch.

The poor guy had lost his taste for his favorite foods,
seen his golf scores nearly double, and now, thanks to New
Moon's ex, lost his manly energies at the full moon.

Jerk face, I thought, proving I was over it. The names I
used to call Mark were a lot more colorful.

New Moon's story ended without fanfare.

Summer and Jade scrambled to course correct with Remus. But the man really was a conspiracy theorist. The closest thing to a werewolf he'd seen was in *An American Werewolf in London*.

Of the five, Evan's story of camping outside Creel Creek was the most believable—although to many listeners it would sound cliche in its "I saw Bigfoot and didn't snap a photo" glory.

Others might wonder how he'd managed to come away from the encounter unscathed.

I questioned it too.

Maybe Other Dave would have an answer.

The episode wrapped up with a roundtable discussion where Remus and Chewbarka did most of the talking.

Aside from her story and the outburst at the beginning of the show, Ginger had stayed tightlipped. Her eyes kept focusing on the exit.

As the show wound down, Simon brought up several bottles of beer and other spirits from downstairs.

When the recording light turned off, he stood outside the studio offering them to the guests as one by one they left the studio space.

Chewbarka waved him off. "Unfortunately, I'm underage."

"Or fortunately," Remus said, smiling. "I'll take his."

Two bottles in hand, the older man sank into the couch where I'd been sitting for the entirety of the show.

Now, I was hovering beside the wall doing my best wall-flower impression.

Evan and Summer joined Remus on the couch. Chewbarka paced the length of the lounge while Jade and the two ladies of the group stored headphones and tidied up the studio.

Without the recording equipment, I couldn't hear what was being said inside, but it was something because Ginger stormed out.

She wasn't sticking around for the after-party.

Neither was New Moon, who brushed past Simon's outstretched hand, nearly knocking the bottle out of it as she rushed through the lounge after Ginger.

I tried to catch them on the stairs, but they were too fast for me. They both exited the building as I made it down to the last step. The door to outside had swung wide open. It crashed to a close, leaving a puff of cold air with it.

I still couldn't hear what the two ladies were talking about. Their raised voices were muffled behind the thick wooden door.

I eased it open and slipped outside.

They were too busy arguing to notice.

Ginger and New Moon had stopped abruptly in the middle of the nearly vacant parking lot. They were between two cars, an older pickup and a Prius. While Ginger seemed to favor the Prius, New Moon leaned in the direction of the pickup.

Between the harsh tones of their voices, and the way their hands flailed about as they talked, there was no mistaking these two were in the midst of an argument that spanned much longer than the last few minutes.

But what are they arguing about?

It had to be Tyson.

Crouching beside Prongs, my Subaru Outback, I eavesdropped, hoping not to draw their attention.

It had gotten colder. There was a chilly bite to the air.

Neither woman seemed to notice or care. They were in

thin T-shirts. I realized they must've left their jackets hanging on the coat rack in the lounge.

With a whispered spell, the jackets popped into my hands. At least now I had a reason to be outside if they caught me.

"You're really just going to leave?" New Moon said. "After... after everything? After all that?"

"All that?" Ginger cried. "That was a disaster."

"No." New Moon shook her head. "The only disaster was you bringing up Tyson."

"The whole thing was a disaster, and you know it. It went exactly like I thought it would—like I told you it would. I just can't believe I was dumb enough to show up. I skipped out on work for... for nothing."

"It's not skipping work if you're still getting paid," New Moon countered.

"I could still get caught."

"But you won't." New Moon kicked at the gravel on the ground. "You never do. Speaking of, you were supposed to call me last night."

"I see what you're doing," Ginger said.

"And that is?"

"Preventing me from leaving."

"Is it working?"

"No." Ginger made an abrupt turn for the Prius.

"I thought we were supposed to be friends," New Moon said, a hint of sadness in her voice. "I could really use one right now."

"You have friends." Ginger motioned in the direction of the brewery. "They're up there. Go be with them."

"They're not my friends." New Moon's eyes followed the gesture. Now, they were both staring in my direction.

It was another second before their eyes landed on me.

Busted.

I stood tall and smoothed the guilt from my face. "I think y'all forgot these."

"Spy much?" Ginger stomped over. She snatched her jacket from my hand.

"Excuse her." New Moon took her leather jacket and eased into it as coolly as a Pink Lady. "It's been a trying week. We lost someone we...well, someone we knew."

Ginger gave her friend a knowing look, meant to be between the two of them. I couldn't decipher its meaning except that Tyson had meant more to them than a screen name they'd chatted with from time-to-time.

"I'm sorry about Tyson," I said. "I didn't realize he was that close to any of you. Evan said you met for the first time last week."

"Yeah, as a group, that's true." New Moon shrugged. "It was the first time we met Evan and Frank and whatever Barky's real name is."

"What about you? How long have you two known each other?"

New Moon raised her eyebrows to Ginger, as if questioning that she could answer me.

Ginger rolled her eyes. "About six months."

"And you're both local?" I asked.

"She is," New Moon answered quickly.

Ginger made a face. That question wasn't supposed to be answered.

"So, did you know Tyson?" It was New Moon's turn to ask.

I shook my head. "I can't say I had the pleasure."

"Who are you anyway?" Ginger took another step toward her car. "A producer or something?"

"Yeah, I'm a producer," I lied.

"Figures." Ginger grunted.

"What's that supposed to mean?"

"It means you're just like those phonies up there. You don't believe us. And you probably think Creel Creek is normal—just like every other small American town."

"I didn't say that." And I never would. Not about Creel Creek.

"You don't have to," she snapped. "It's written all over your pretty face."

"I didn't mean to offend you," I said.

"It wasn't you," she said. "Not really. It was your talent. Athena, or should I say Summer. It's funny. I've heard that saying about never meeting your idols like a thousand times. Well, Athena and Ivana were never my idols. At first, I thought they were kind of a joke. And they still were able to disappoint me. They didn't believe a word we said."

"Don't." New Moon put up a hand, but it was too late.

Ginger barreled on. "I tried to tell you. I said they were fakes. They don't care about the paranormal world or the magic or anything. Maybe they used to, but now they're jaded."

In more ways than one.

"And no offense, but so are you." Ginger's statement didn't sting me quite as bad.

I was jaded.

I had magic in my fingertips, but nothing I did seemed to work out as I expected.

Or wanted.

Ginger was right about the podcast too. Since becoming a witch herself, Summer hadn't cared for it much. She'd let it fall into disrepair. And she'd actively worked against revealing magical secrets to the wide world.

Then there was Jade. She hadn't been herself—not since, well, not since she wasn't herself.

New Moon winced in my direction, as if I really was a producer of the show and might share these grievances with Summer and Jade.

"They were nice enough," she said.

"Were they though?" Sarcasm dripped from Ginger's voice. "How can you say that?"

"They were nice about Tyson," New Moon offered. "They didn't have to be."

"That was my mistake. I shouldn't have brought him up."

"Speaking of, can you tell me a little about Tyson?" I was afraid they'd think it was for the podcast. "This isn't for the show. I'm just genuinely curious. From what Evan said, Tyson didn't exactly line up with his online persona."

"Listen, whoever you are," Ginger said. "It's late and it's cold. Maybe we can do this another time?"

"Agreed. I think we should go." New Moon took a step toward the pickup.

The lie had turned on me. They had to understand I wasn't after information just for information's sake.

I wanted—I needed—to solve this mystery.

Both Ginger and New Moon turned to leave.

Something came over me. Magic hummed in the back of my throat. I could feel it. And I knew exactly what I had to do.

I had to say the magic word.

If I did, they would tell me everything I needed to know.

But how is this possible?

You're a witch, a voice, but not my own, echoed in my mind. *Anything's possible with magic.*

"Please," I said, the magic word eliciting some real magic. "Just five more minutes? Tell me about Tyson."

25

THE CASE AGAINST TYSON BRIGGS

"This is going to take a lot more than five minutes," New Moon said.

"Plus, I'm freezing," Ginger added. "Is there anywhere else we can go?"

"We can go back inside." I was cold too. The difference being I was willing to freeze for some answers.

"Anywhere but there." Ginger's face puckered. "If I never see that Remus creeper again, it'll be too soon."

"Too soon," New Moon agreed.

It was late, and there weren't many options. I racked my brain for an answer. "I guess I could open up the bookstore..."

"I knew you looked familiar," Ginger said. "You work there, don't you?"

"I do."

Although I didn't remember her. Probably because my memory wasn't what it used to be. That and the store had quite the influx of customers over the past year.

New Moon adjusted her glasses. "Technically, we're banned from there."

"Right." Ginger winced. "I wouldn't be surprised if we lost all our hair if we went back. Remember, that happened to Athena Hunter a while back?"

"You're not getting cursed tonight."

Ginger snorted. "Non-believers."

"I'm a witch." I don't know why it felt like defending myself by outing my secret was the smart play. But again, it was late. I was tired and fed up for a number of reasons.

Ginger raised an eyebrow. "Seriously? Well, if that's the case, then we'll meet you there. Just promise us we'll have hair in the end."

"Girl Scouts' honor," I said.

Although I couldn't promise there'd be no curse.

Trish's go-to hex had changed since the run-in with Summer several years ago. Now, she liked to turn the victim's hair neon green.

It wouldn't be instantaneous like it had been on Summer. It was a much more subtle spell—the hair changed shade over the course of several weeks, making it much harder to trace the spell's lineage.

Their cars followed mine down the road to the strip mall that was now solely Bewitched Books. The cafe lights were dimmed and aglow. Otherwise, the store was pitch-black.

I unlocked the front and went to the cafe to put on coffee. It was one of those nights when I wasn't going to get much sleep anyway.

I'd have to try to catch a few hours while the girls were at school.

As the two women entered the store, a burst of magical energy filtered in with them, just as they crossed the threshold.

Remind me to ask Trish to cancel out that spell, I thought.

"*Will do,*" Twinkie said. The mouse scurried out of a cabinet as I reached for a bag of coffee beans.

What were you doing in here?

"*Needed a pick-me-up,*" she replied.

Don't we all.

"I don't think we had proper introductions before," I said. "I'm Constance. Constance Campbell."

I waited for their names—their real names—and New Moon was on the cusp of telling me hers when Ginger grabbed her by the shoulder. "Nuh uh. We'll tell her about Tyson, but not about us."

New Moon pressed her lips together and smiled a polite apology.

"Fine." I sighed. "If that's how it's going to be."

"And you can't put any of this on the show," Ginger reminded me.

They were still under the impression I produced *Creel Creek After Dark*.

"I wouldn't dream of it."

They settled at a table beside the window. With the lighting, about anyone could look in and see us inside. But the likelihood of someone passing by at this time of night was slim.

"Hot chocolate or coffee?" I asked.

"Coffee for me," Ginger said. "I work the late shift."

"When you work," New Moon quipped.

"We need to make this quick," Ginger added. "I have to get home before my roommate leaves for work."

"They work the same job," New Moon said.

"Which is?"

"We're answering questions about Tyson," she reminded me.

I groaned, then finished making their drinks and joined them.

Outside the window, Main Street's singular lamppost lit a small patch of asphalt. Behind it, invisible in the darkness, stood the remnants of the county courthouse.

Despite several threats of it being torn down and replaced, the burnt-out shell remained an eyesore. Inside, it held a portal opening to the shadow realm—the world between our world and every other.

Ginger took a sip of her coffee. "What do you want to know?"

I shrugged. "Everything?"

"Like?" Ginger wasn't willing to just tell me their story. Not from the start.

"Like how you two knew Tyson outside of the chat?"

"I guess that means you want to hear how he catfished us for a year before we learned who he really was."

"Ginger!" New Moon complained.

"It's fine," she said. "I just don't want Constance thinking Tyson was some sort of victim."

"He was murdered," I said.

"He was attacked by a werewolf. There's a difference."

"The evidence doesn't support that," I said and looked to New Moon for backup that didn't come.

"Well, we weren't privy to any evidence."

New Moon's eyes stayed fixed inside her mug. "Tyson was dating—online dating—both of us. Only he didn't know we were friends outside of the chat. When he found that out, instead of coming clean, he tried to play us against each other."

"And you were still dating him?"

"We weren't like really dating," New Moon said. "We were talking."

"Maybe you'd like to see all of our texts and private convos?"

"Ginger!"

"What?" she scoffed. "I don't even know what we're doing here. Or why we agreed to come. Tell us, if it's not for the show, then why do you care about Tyson?"

I was tired of lying. It was better to just be honest. "Because someone I care about was framed for the murder."

"You mean a werewolf?" Ginger raised an eyebrow.

"Someone you care about is a werewolf?" New Moon lifted her chin.

I nodded.

More than one someone.

"So, you don't have to believe us," Ginger said. "Because you already know."

I nodded again. "And I also know this werewolf didn't kill Tyson. Something, or someone else, did."

New Moon tipped her glasses up to her brow. "You're probably thinking we killed him. That we have motive. But we didn't—we didn't want him to die."

"He was an ass though," Ginger said.

"A big one," New Moon agreed. "Especially *after* we met him here."

"After?" I questioned. "Does that mean you... you saw him after everything that happened in the bookstore?"

"Unfortunately," Ginger said morosely.

"What happened?"

New Moon looked to Ginger for confirmation she could speak, and the woman with the cat eye glasses nodded. "He followed us to Ginger's house is what happened."

"And?"

"And we didn't kill him," Ginger said.

"But we did scare him a little," New Moon said.

"How?"

I wasn't going to find out. Headlights appeared on the street. As they eased toward the store, cold blue lights flashed above them.

My heart stopped. I had to remind myself I wasn't doing anything wrong.

For a moment, I thought it might be Mac on a patrol. Maybe he was finally going to have a talk with these two.

But it was worse.

Dave, not Dave, stepped out of his SUV.

"It's the cops," Ginger whispered.

"No," I said. "It's my sort of boyfriend."

26

CONSTANCE CAMPBELL AND THE
MORPHING MEN

While dating might've gotten Tyson into trouble, it probably wasn't what got him killed. Neither Ginger nor New Moon seemed the type. Granted, I'd been fooled by stone-cold killers before.

I wasn't going to rule them out entirely.

But maybe Tyson had broken a few more hearts along the way.

Tonight, I had my own heart to worry about.

It took some convincing, most of it at the bookstore after explaining why it was open in the dead of night, but I finally broke down and agreed to a date night with Other Dave.

In Creel Creek, a mere handful of restaurants were what I considered date-worthy. There was a Thai restaurant, Tasty Thai, and a Mexican place called Los Bravos. Although Dave tended not to stretch his culinary palate too far. He liked the chain restaurant Orange Blossoms, which had a tiny bar, polite employees, and a menu that rivaled most textbooks in size and complication.

How many ways are there to make a hamburger? According to the Orange Blossoms menu, well over fifty.

"Table for two, please."

"Uh, yeah, it's Friday. We have your usual, Sheriff." The hostess had picked up on Dave's awkward demeanor faster than me.

She led us to our table.

Our table.

Being here with this other version of him felt wrong.

Other Dave took in the surroundings with a smug smile. It was Dave's smile, and I couldn't remember a single time he'd worn it like that.

He'd gotten his way—this date with me—mostly because I was hoping he knew more about the murder investigation.

Then there was the promise of speaking to the real Dave.

"This place is nice," he said.

It wasn't.

Orange Blossoms wasn't much to look at. To be more fair, we'd both played a part in its demise. A monster from the shadow realm attacked us one date night in the past.

For some strange reason, the encounter wasn't covered by the restaurant's insurance. A local GoFundMe had raised the money for the repairs. But the silly decorations that had once adorned the walls were never replaced. The walls were mostly bare and painted an awful shade of orange.

"So, this is what you two do for fun?" Other Dave leaned his chair back. "You pay someone to cook food for you when you have plenty of food in the kitchen? A kitchen that, by the way, is a mere thirty-three feet from the bedroom."

"A bedroom you're not sleeping in tonight," I said.

"Why's that? Because you didn't sleep much in it last night."

"I was busy," I said.

"I know. But you not being in bed is why I drove around town looking for you."

"I thought you were just working late?"

He shook his head. "What were you talking about with those ladies?"

"Trying to help," I said. "Trying to figure out who murdered Tyson."

"That's good. I bet you're making better headway than Mac. That guy seems to be finding dead end after dead end."

"And you're working the other case, right?" I asked.

He nodded. "In fact, you met our suspect."

"Maude?" I was surprised but not very. There was something strange about that old woman.

"I just need a few more things to fall into place, and we'll have her."

"What will that mean exactly?"

He shrugged. "Proof. Proof that Dad didn't do what he thought he did."

"Are you going to tell him?"

"Tell him what?" Dave's brow furrowed.

"I don't know—that he's not the killer he thought he was?"

"I would tell him, but I can't reach him. He doesn't exactly have a phone."

"Seriously?"

Other Dave smiled. It was more akin to the smile I was used to. "I don't think so. And your Dave agrees. He says Dad didn't believe in technology back when technology was a TV and a rotary phone in the kitchen. Guaranteed, he doesn't have a cell phone now."

"You could go see him," I offered. "If you knew where he lived..."

From my conversation with Imogene, I was pretty sure Dave didn't know.

"I know where he lives," he said.

"You do?" I was puzzled.

He nodded, grinning. "Well, not exactly. But I know he lives in a werewolf community up north."

"A community of werewolves... really?"

"Something like that," he said. "It's supposed to be a place for wolves to be wolves. To let the other guy out, no matter the phase of the moon. I remember he called it Lycanthropia. But the way he talked about it, I was never sure if it was a myth or a dream or something else."

"But it's real?"

"Let's just say, even if it was a myth, it won't be anymore. Dad's had twenty years to turn his vision into a reality."

"Interesting," I said.

But it worried me. Maybe this was like Other Dave's quest. Maybe he had to tell his father that he was innocent. There was just about a week left before the next full moon when I would hopefully be rid of this version of Dave for good.

"What else happens on dates?" Other Dave asked. "I know what I've seen in movies and TV."

"Are you asking if I'm going to kiss you on this date?"

"We could hold hands..."

"I'm not going to hold your hand."

"Fine. Then what do you two talk about? What exactly do you and Dave have in common?"

"I don't know," I said, frustrated. "We talk about work. About the girls. Random stuff like movies and TV shows. We usually talk about what we want to watch that night."

"What do you want to watch tonight?"

"Nothing with you," I said.

"You're being rather mean, and I haven't done anything to deserve it."

Except exist.

I gathered my purse. "I can just leave now, if you want."

"Before we eat our traditional bread basket?" He put his hand atop mine to stop me. A tingle of recognition ran down my arm.

This isn't our Dave.

"That oil and balsamic vinegar," he continued. "I've heard good things."

I scowled. "How do you know about that?"

"Lucky guess?" He tapped the second page of the menu. "Or maybe, some guy is occupying a part of my head. Plus, when you're around, he doesn't seem to shut up. No matter how much I threaten to lock him away."

"Dave?"

"That's right. You want to talk to him."

I gave him a short nod. "Please?"

"Too bad." The magic word didn't have the effect it had the night before.

"I knew you were lying."

"Not lying. I'll let you talk to him... eventually."

I went to roll my eyes but found the queen of the eye-roll was already in the room. Trish's purple tipped hair covered her left cheek. She sat in a booth across from a beautiful blonde woman.

I watched, momentarily transfixed, but not nearly as much as they were with each other. Trish's gaze hadn't moved away from the blonde's inky black-eyed stare.

That was how a date night should be. The focus on each other—not on the food or on a phone in your hand.

"Who's that?" Other Dave interrupted my thoughts.

"Trish," I said.

"Oh." He nodded as the waitress delivered the bread. "And I believe you know this woman at the bar, too?"

"Why do you say that?"

"Because she keeps waving at you."

I turned to find Summer Shields tipping a cocktail up in the air. The chair beside her was empty.

"That's right. She wants me to meet her boyfriend, so don't be surprised when they want to join us for dinner."

"And you're okay with that?"

"Tonight, I am," I said.

"So, is this trap?" Hesitantly, Dave dipped bread into the oil. "Dave warned me you might try to have the other witches help you with a spell."

"Not at Orange Blossoms," I said.

But as the words came tumbling out, I saw another witch in the corner booth. Kalene. A man in a ten-gallon hat sat opposite to her.

I couldn't help but count the witches again. Summer, alone at the bar. Trish, whose date must've gone to the bathroom. And now, Kalene.

Good thing Lauren lived in another town. Otherwise, this really could be an ambush.

After nibbling on several slices of bread, I felt a tap on my shoulder. Summer smiled down. "Constance, there's someone I'd like you to meet. This is Carver."

"How do you do?" A tall man in a neat sport coat clasped my fingertips and pressed his lips to the backside of my hand. He had jet-black eyes and nearly perfect features.

He reminded me of someone, but someone I couldn't place.

"Carver." Other Dave stood and reached out a hand. "It's nice to meet you. Would y'all like to sit? We were just about to order."

"No, we don't want to impose," Carver said.

"We'd love to." Summer beamed, but poor Carver looked put out. Maybe he wanted some alone time on their one-month anniversary.

"Fine," he said. "You go ahead. I'm just going to run to the bathroom real quick."

It was a popular place. I noticed Kalene's date was now gone, and Trish's returned as Summer got settled.

"So, what do you think? He's cute right?"

"Very handsome," I said.

"You know I'm still here, right? And Dave can hear you too."

"Dave's understanding. I can call another man handsome. But if he's upset, maybe you should let me talk to him.'"

"That's a slippery slope I'm not going down. Not tonight anyway. How are you, Summer? We haven't been formally introduced. I'm—"

"The wolf." Summer leaned in closer. "I think it's kinda hot, you and Dave switching places."

"I know, right? Who wouldn't want this?" Dave waved his hand around his chest.

"What'd I miss?" Carver asked, getting seated.

"Not much," Dave answered. "We were just discussing how I'm not exactly what I seem. But neither are you, are you Carver?"

"Come again?" Carver asked.

"What's this about?" Summer asked.

I struggled a moment too. Then I looked again at Trish's table. Her date was missing. So was Kalene's.

My subconscious understood something was wrong, but I hadn't put it together like Dave had.

"I think what Dave is trying to say," I said, "is you're all dating the same—the same something."

Carver's beady black eyes darted around the room, checking every deserted table, as if the other witches might've caught on at the same time.

They hadn't.

"I guess that's my cue." A mischievous smile etched across Carver's face. And in a puff of black smoke, he disappeared, leaving an empty seat and an astonished dining room.

AFTER WE SORTED things out with the witches and wiped the memories of most patrons, Dave insisted on our traditional molten chocolate lava cake.

I wasn't hungry. A first. I watched him devour it. "You know, at first, I didn't understand the whole carbs thing. Now, I think I could live off carbs alone," he said.

"You'd think that." I rolled my eyes.

"What's wrong?"

"Uh, you were here. You know what's wrong."

"It's not like you were dating that thing."

"But my friends were," I said. "And I don't like dealing in things I don't know about. What the heck was that?"

He pursed his lips. "Not sure. This is my first rodeo, so to speak. Your Dave says he doesn't have a clue either. I will say it was entertaining. You ready to go home?"

"I am," I said. "But you're not going there with me."

"I'm not?" His thick eyebrows knitted.

"No. You're staying somewhere else tonight. I'll drive."

Dave sat shotgun as I maneuvered his SUV toward

Gran's house. "I'd say I don't like mysteries, but I don't think it's accurate."

"You like them?"

"A part of me does. A part of us, I should say. Speaking of, I was kind of thinking when all that crazy was going down."

"About?"

"I think it might be easier to wrap up this case if I talk to Dad."

"I thought you wanted things to fall into place?"

"Yeah, well, they might not if I don't talk to him and get the full story."

"So, what I'm hearing is you want to go see your father."

"Our father." He nodded.

"Who lives in some mythical place. Any idea where it is?"

I could tell Dave was gearing up to say something I wouldn't like. "That's kind of the problem. I have no clue."

I turned down Gran's street, then pulled into her driveway where Prongs was conveniently parked outside. Mom and I had planned this earlier.

We sat in the driveway, the car idling.

"So, your dad never hinted at its location?" I asked.

"He might've, but I don't remember. We don't remember. You'd think if something like this existed there'd be rumblings. Someone in the shifter community would know about it."

"If only there was a place that knew the comings and goings of shifters," I said sarcastically.

"Was that sarcasm? Does such a place exist?"

"I guess Dave hasn't told you about the league then?"

"Never mentioned it."

"I'll take you there tomorrow," I said. "I'll take you on one condition."

"You get to speak to Dave?" He inclined his head.

"That's the one."

"Deal," he said. "Now, what about a kiss goodnight?"

"In your dreams, wolf boy."

In about a second flat, I was out of his car and inside Prongs, screeching away from the driveway.

27

THE HOUSE GUEST

OTHER DAVE

From the front porch steps, I watched the lights of Constance's Subaru fade into the distance, and a pang of something settled into the pit of my stomach.

It's called longing, dude. Get used to it.

"What do you know about it?" I groused.

I dug into my jeans' pocket for the key Constance had given me in the car. The keychain had a rubber ducky on it. Its cuteness somehow added to that weird feeling.

You like her. You might even love her.

"Well, she's gorgeous—what's not to like?"

It's more than that, and you know it.

"Can you shut up for a second? I think I hear something."

There were sounds coming from inside the empty house. And they weren't small sounds either. I jiggled open the door and allowed it to open wide.

Whatever it was—whoever it was—didn't scare me.

Nothing scared me.

You aren't the wolf right now. Someone stabs you with a knife, you bleed to death, and you die.

"We bleed to death, and we die," I corrected.

Fair point. Grab that lamp and hold it like a baseball bat.

"What's a baseball bat?"

Just grab it.

The house was so dark. Dave's stupid eyes were no help. I flipped a few light switches, finding a dusty living room with a couch, a recliner, and a decent size TV.

The room opened up to a kitchen on the other side. But I couldn't see much more than a refrigerator and a bit of countertop.

The loud rustling of some sort of bag pricked my ears again. Maybe those loud sounds I'd heard weren't that loud after all.

Maybe a rat had found its way into the kitchen and was eating through the pantry.

Gross.

"Oh, so, a rat scares you?"

Shut up.

"I'm trying to get you to. What do you think, Dave? Is it safe?"

Do what you want, he answered.

I strode through the living room, my steps heavy on the carpet. Inside the kitchen, I found another row of light switches and threw them on.

For a brief moment, my body tensed out of some human reflex, ready for a small rodent to run across its path.

Nothing to be scared of.

Except there wasn't a small rodent in the kitchen.

A rather large raccoon was helping itself to an open bag

of cat food. There was a bowl beside it, filled with kibble. A big black cat paused its meal, yellow eyes fixed on me.

"Huh." I shook my head.

Constance hadn't mentioned any house guests. But a quick perusal of Dave's memory banks told me who these creatures were.

"Familiars," I said, as if they didn't know what they were. "It's not fair. You can understand me, but I won't be able to understand you. Especially now that we're roommates. I'm Dave, by the way. But not the Dave you know."

They can read your mind, dummy. It's probably how Constance knew you were an imposter.

"Right." I preferred to speak to them. As Dave knew, I wasn't good with thoughts. "Anyway," I told them. "Constance is making me sleep here tonight. She wants some time alone. I'm never alone, am I, Dave?"

Dave didn't answer. Maybe he preferred to shield his thoughts from the familiars.

I doubted they were interested. I just wished they could communicate back.

As if reading my mind—which they totally could—someone cursed loudly.

It took me a moment to realize the voice hadn't come from the kitchen. It came from just outside it.

Then the back door swung open.

A man—at least I thought it was a man—stepped inside. He shivered from the cold and cursed again. "It's freezing out."

His eyes glanced off me, went to the familiars, then he did a double take. "What the hell are you doing here?"

My brain was even slower processing. "Nothing?"

"D<small>AVE</small>," he said. "*The* Dave. We met earlier."

"I don't believe we have," I said.

"Oh, but we did. You ruined a rather fun game for me." The man threw off his jacket and flung it on a coat rack beside the back door.

He had slick black hair and wore a black linen shirt, black pants, and shiny black shoes. Everything about his appearance was neat and tidy. His cheeks were chiseled and smooth. His eyes were jet black too—the same as every witch's date in the restaurant.

"It's you," I said.

"Yeah, it's me." He nodded. "From Orange Blossoms. You're a clever chap. Glad I got out of there before your girl recognized me."

"Who are you?" I asked him.

"The name's Custos," he said. "And you—you're the wolf. These two have told me all about you."

"You can talk to them?"

"I'm a demon. Of course I can. I can do a lot more than that."

"A demon. Like from—"

"From there, yeah. I'm up here now though—out on good behavior."

"You call what happened tonight good behavior?"

"Breaking hearts isn't nearly as bad as sending monsters out in the world, is it? Humans do both. Sometimes worse."

Custos began prying his fingers into his eyes. When he was done, he held a pair of contacts in his hand, and his eyes had turned a shade of crimson. "The only color that blocks out the red."

"What are you doing here?" I asked him.

"Living my best life. Isn't that what we're all striving for?"

"I'm just trying to find a life," I said.

"It's tough. Being a part of some big whole you never agreed to. I get it. I do. It's the reason Stevie's here now. Come to ask me a few questions. I'm like one of those, what do you call it—"

"I'm not good at that game," I told him.

"Yeah, well, you wouldn't be."

I tried not to take offense at the comment.

"Anyway, if you want to grab a beer from the fridge and veg out with us for a few episodes of *Lucifer*, you're more than welcome."

It didn't sound like the worst idea.

28

THE MOON'S CURSE

The League of Artemis was a fraternal order, uniting shifters from around the globe. Most shifters of Creel Creek, including Dave, were members.

Reminiscent of a masonry temple, their den was a squat building on the outskirts of town with little signage.

An etched symbol above the door reminded me of a cave drawing. It was three sets of paws, each inside the other with the largest paw, something like that of a bear, on the outside.

We knocked on the door, and an older woman answered. She was thin. Her short gray hair had patches of sandy brown. Her driver's license probably claimed she had brown eyes when they were truly a golden color.

I knew her well.

Helen Pratt was Imogene's mother-in-law. She'd taken over duties as a league elder after a few others had come to a gruesome demise.

She wrapped me in a hug. "It's been a while. I got your

text to be here, but why are y'all knocking? Dave should have a key."

"This isn't really Dave," I said.

"I see." She gave him a once over but didn't ask for further explanation.

Inside, the common area was more like a large bar with ample amounts of seating. From this room, the building split off into two sections. To our left were offices, a kitchen, and other small rooms. To our right, there was a hallway leading down to an underground chamber below our feet.

The temple room was where most league business was carried out, and it was done in shifted form. Dave carried an amulet that allowed him to change into wolf form but maintain his rational self, so I understood why he'd wanted to keep the league a secret from his wolf counterpart.

With the amulet, he could shift at any time. He could be helpful and not blood thirsty.

I was happy when Helen led us toward her office. It meant, for now, this chat would be just that, without formal league protocols.

Her office was larger than I thought it'd be. There was a couch and a few chairs opposite a massive wooden desk. The chair behind it would be suitable for the Oval Office. It filled this space with a grandeur I wasn't expecting after our short walk down the dingy hallway.

Nor was I expecting to find someone else seated in the room.

"Dave." The woman nodded.

"This is my daughter, Tori," Helen said.

Like her mother, Tori was thin but nearly a head taller. She had long reddish-brown hair. It was the same color when she shifted into her coyote form.

"Mom." Tori shook her head. "We've met. It's been a while, Constance. How are you?"

"I've been better," I said.

"Oh, so this isn't a happy visit?"

"Is it ever?" Helen plopped into her grand office chair. "You said before this *isn't* really Dave. If it's not him, then who is it?"

"It's... it's the—"

"Wolf," Helen finished.

"I'm right here," Other Dave said. "And so is Dave, by the way."

"Oh, wow! Mom, do you think he's been Moon Cursed?"

"Moon Cursed?"

Tori smiled. "It's what they call it when his innie becomes his outtie and his outtie becomes his innie. I've heard it happens to all werewolves at least once in their lifetime. Bad luck for Dave it happened now."

"There's no such thing as luck," Helen said. "Especially when you're dealing with a goddess. She did this for a reason."

"I don't know." Tori chewed her lip. "I don't think the gods use logic—at least that's the view from my cheap seats."

"I said she had a reason," Helen argued. "I never said it was logical. And if you're in the cheap seats, then I guess I'm up in the rafters."

"If that's the case, where does that put me?" I asked.

"Oh, you're on the field or the court or whatever," Tori said. "Remind me again why we're doing sports metaphors? I hate sports."

"That's funny," I said. "You look like you'd be good at them."

"Climbing. Six days a week, every week since I was, what, thirteen?"

"You were climbing trees well before then." Helen gazed out the window of the room. It was easy to see her mind was elsewhere. Probably off with Tori climbing a tree some thirty years ago.

"I guess you've come looking for help," Tori said. "Mom, do you know any remedies for this?"

"There are none," she answered. "It has to go away on its own."

"Again, I'm here in the room," Other Dave said.

"And that's not exactly why we're here."

Helen swiveled her chair around. "I knew it was something else."

"What is it?" Tori asked.

I nudged Other Dave in the side. "Go ahead, Mister I'm Still in the Room."

Other Dave explained about his father and this mythical Lycanthropia he'd planned to build. The ladies listened, nodding along and not asking many questions.

"The problem," Other Dave said, "is I have no clue where this place is."

"If it even exists," I added.

"Oh, it exists," Helen said. "I can't say I know the exact latitude and longitude, but I do have a general idea. The thing is, I thought you and Imogene hated your father?"

"They might," Other Dave said.

"But not you." She pressed her lips together.

"And what you need to talk to him about, it's that important?" Tori chewed her lip again, but this time, it wasn't playfully.

"It's important." Other Dave was more serious than I'd

seen him. It reminded me of my Dave, who I still hadn't gotten the chance to speak with.

"It wouldn't be an easy journey. It's about as far away from civilization as a place can get. Up in Canada. You'd probably have to make a trip to Winnipeg or Toronto, then find some other means of travel to get up there. We're likely talking days of travel, and it's, what, about a week until the full moon. I don't think Constance would want to be there then, if you catch my drift."

"Not a problem," Other Dave said. "Dave says he has some SkyMiles we can trade in."

I laughed at the lie. "The ones he's been saving for a trip to Hawaii? You really are a piece of work."

"I'll get you the details," Helen said. "How you make the trip is up to you two."

"I'm not going with him," I said.

Helen popped out of her chair. "I hate to say it, but I think you should."

"Why's that?"

"The goddess again," Tori answered. "She did this for a reason. You two are meant to be together."

I hate magic.

"At least think about it," Helen said.

She led us out, finding Dave a dusty map from a storage closet and charting it out with the approximate location of this Lycanthropia place.

At the threshold, she squeezed me into another hug. "I guess now is as good a time as any to tell you I'm leaving Creel Creek. Tori's taking over my seat as Elder."

"Where are you going?" I asked.

"Just down the street from Imogene and Jared." She smiled. "Nana can't stand being away from her grandbabies. Even if they aren't exactly babies anymore."

"I get it," I said. "We miss them something fierce. The girls can't wait to visit this summer. They need their cousin time."

"I'm sure they do," she said. "So, I'll be seeing you. In the meantime, if you need anything else from the shifter community—and I do mean anything—ask Tori. She's here to help."

"I will," I said.

But I hoped I'd never take her up on that offer.

"I guess this means you're Moon Cursed, whatever that is."

Dave settled into the passenger seat. "We're Moon Cursed. Me and Dave, that is. He disagrees with Mrs. Pratt. He says you're not connected like that. Also, he doesn't think you should go with me. If you want to talk to him, you can."

"What do you think?" I asked.

The face of the handsome man beside me went blank. "You're asking me?"

"Yeah, what do you think? Are we connected or not?"

"I think Dave's been fighting something."

"Like?"

"His connection with you."

"So, you're saying we are connected." I didn't know what to say or do. I wanted to talk to Dave, but a part of me wanted to know more about this curse.

"He really wants to talk to you," Other Dave said.

"I'm sure he does."

"And I promised you could…"

"You did." I laughed to myself. "What does he really say about using his SkyMiles?"

"Uh, that he'll kill me if I do."

"I'd hate for that to happen, since technically you're both the same person."

"Technically, we are." He nodded. "Constance, I have to do this. I have to find our dad."

"I understand."

"And you'll keep the girls?"

"My mom will."

Dave's eyebrow crept up his forehead. "Does that mean what I think it means?"

I waited a beat to answer. Surely my body was going to tell me how stupid I was being. This wasn't a good idea. I should back out now.

But it was the opposite. The same weird feeling I'd had when asking Ginger and New Moon to talk about Tyson lingered in the back of my head.

Instead of answering, I asked him, "How do you plan to explain this to Mac?"

"I'm still the sheriff," Other Dave said. "Mac reports to me."

"So, you're not going to tell him?"

He broke into a true grin. "I'm not going to tell him."

29

THE WEREWOLF PLACE

The town was about as remote as it could be. Situated in the lower reaches of the Nunavut territory, it was only reachable by ski plane this time of year.

After a few failed attempts, I wasn't sure we'd find a pilot willing to make the trip.

But we finally did.

Other Dave, with Dave's help, negotiated with a bear shifter named Gavin Bouchard who was already delivering a shipment of supplies to a town even farther north.

Probably full of polar bear shifters, I thought.

It was a small plane, a single engine, and Gavin had us help with the pre-flight checklist before we crammed inside along with the cargo.

"Is someone expecting you up there?" Gavin asked.

"Not exactly," Other Dave answered.

"Way I hear it, those folks don't take too kind to strangers."

"I'm sure you've heard lots of things about this place,"

Other Dave yelled over the plane noise. "Doesn't mean they're all true."

"All I'm saying is I'm not looking for trouble."

"We understand," Other Dave said.

"It's in and out for me." Gavin began checking dials in the cockpit. "I'll give you the number to my sat phone. Then I can pick you up in a couple of days when I head south again."

"What if we need you sooner?" Dave's wary gaze fell on me.

There were a lot of unknowns in this trip. Getting dropped off in the middle-of-nowhere Canada with nowhere to stay and the temperatures below freezing wasn't exactly ideal.

But what other choice did we have?

"Couple of days. Maybe a week." Gavin cranked up the engine, and he didn't seem to hear or care to hear any of Dave's yelled responses.

But he did hand us some headsets before takeoff.

The flight was uneventful and loud. Even with my headset on, I couldn't understand Gavin's garbled speech as he pointed out the landmarks we were flying over.

Most of the ground was covered in snow.

The bush pilot made several calls over the radio throughout the journey to the local air traffic control. But there wasn't a tower close. Or an airport for that matter.

He landed on a field of snow.

"The town's about a half mile that way." He pointed, never shutting off the engine as we hefted our things into the snow.

I don't know what I expected from Lycanthropia but this wasn't it. It was a quaint small town. It screamed Canada, which in many ways meant it looked a lot like an American town of the late nineteen-eighties. There was a main drag, not exactly a road, but it was paved and plowed of snow. The town boasted a post office and a bowling alley.

A movie rental store caught my eye. Its sign had a familiar color scheme of blue and yellow, but the name didn't ring any bells—Fetch's Flicks.

"Maybe we should go inside and ask around?"

Other Dave, who'd hefted our bags over his shoulders, shook his head. "They're all closed."

"That seems like a bad sign."

"Nah, it's Sunday."

"I don't see a hotel," I said.

"Me neither."

Other Dave continued his slow march up the street. Meanwhile, I was freezing to death in my eight or nine layers. I wasted the last of my hot hands on the plane. They'd warm up for a second or two before petering out again.

Every now and then, my teeth would start chattering, and I had to spell them to stop.

"You hear that?" He turned and walked backwards. He didn't seem to have a care in the world about the snow or the possibility of ice he might slip on.

"No?" But I was a good twenty feet behind him.

I picked up the pace. Then I heard it, the rhythmic sound of someone chopping wood.

"This way." Other Dave meandered over to a smaller path leading away from the gaggle of shops to where several small cabins were lined in a row.

He came to an abrupt stop, letting our bags fall to the ground at his feet.

At the last cabin, there was a man outside chopping wood. I couldn't make out his features.

Other Dave stood there for a long moment, as if he were frozen. As if he didn't know what to do or say.

"It's him," he whispered softly.

He watched the man chop another log before approaching the fence.

Dave's father was taller than Dave. He was lanky, with a pot belly stretching the seams of his rust-colored bib pants. A jacket of a similar color lay neatly over the fence, as if he'd taken it off after working up a good sweat with the ax.

His father had grown a long and shaggy beard. Like his hair, it was as white as the snow covering the ground.

Dave cleared his throat. "Hello?"

The man didn't seem to hear well.

Without looking our way, he grabbed another log and set it atop the stump.

This time, when he turned, I caught a glimpse of something attached to his ears. I tapped Dave on the shoulder, then motioned to my ears. "Hearing aids?"

Dave contemplated a moment, then he improvised. He bent down, made a snowball, and before I could stop him, hurled it at his father's face.

It hit the man square in the mouth, snowflakes flying everywhere and catching in the long beard.

For a second, I was afraid—afraid he was going to be angry.

Then a smile broke from inside the beard. His cheeks flushed. Even his eyes got in on the game, twinkling with a warmth I would never have expected.

The picture I had of this man came from Dave's words, most of them harsh. Dave had built his father up as a bigot who made crude jokes about other paranormals like vampires and witches. He was someone who never cared much for his family, including Dave's mother.

My brain had done a paint by numbers, making the man in my head as opposite to Dave as someone could be. In reality, they favored each other much more than they differed.

Dave had his father's deep set eyes. Their noses were similar, although his father's was more bulbous at the tip.

His father glanced up, searching for his snowball attacker. But when he found Dave with his arm still outstretched from the throw, the grin vanished. He looked as if he'd seen a ghost, or more accurately, a person he never thought he would see again.

"Dave?" He fiddled with his hearing aids.

"It's me, Dad."

"Yeah, I can see that."

"No, Dad." Other Dave shook his head. "It's *me*."

The older man squinted. He strode across the yard and gripped Dave's shoulders. Stared into the dark eyes of his son.

"How is that possible?" he asked. "Unless... unless you've merged?"

"No, Dad. We haven't merged."

"Then how?"

Other Dave smiled weakly. "Maybe you'd like to invite us inside? We can talk about it..."

"Yes. Of course." His father peeked around Dave, his eyes glinting in the sun. "Who is this pretty thing you've brought with you?"

"A friend," Dave said.

Friend? Really?

I'd been demoted. But by which Dave? Maybe both.

"Jack Marsters." Dave's father reached out a hand. "Any friend of Dave's is a friend of mine."

"Constance," I said. "Constance Campbell."

Former longtime girlfriend of your son.

"Well, Constance, it's good to meet you. Let's get inside where it's warm. I doubt you're used to cold like this."

"Is anyone?"

He laughed, but it was an honest question.

How anyone could get used to this climate defied all logic. I was frozen solid since our flight landed in Toronto. The puddle jumping flights that followed had minuscule heaters, which did nothing except prevent our noses from getting frostbite.

Jack scooped an armful of logs and led us inside his cabin.

Like the rest of town, it was small and cozy. A fireplace roared beside a furry rug, made of something looking a whole lot like a reindeer hide. The couch and chairs were stitched with similar material.

Like the exterior of the cabin, the interior walls were rustic. An exposed beam ran the length of the room, along with the trusses.

Jack threw a log on the fire and set aside the others. "Go ahead. Take those coats off and get close to the fire. I'll alert the missus."

I didn't need the encouragement. I thawed out like a pot roast after spending a few years in the bottom of a freezer.

A voice—a female voice—called out from somewhere inside the cabin, "Is that you, Jack? Who are you talking to?"

"You're not going to believe it, but we have company tonight."

His personality didn't match what I'd pictured of Dave's father either. This man seemed so nice. He was almost jovial.

A woman with long gray braids rounded a corner into the den. She held a wooden spoon.

But she wasn't brandishing it as a weapon. She'd come from the kitchen. It was held level with a practiced and steady hand. She gave us a warm smile before shoving the spoon toward Jack's mouth. "Try it. What do you think?"

He obliged with a grin. "Delicious as usual."

"You're sure it doesn't need more salt?"

"If you put any more salt in that, I'll be floating in my bubble baths. Is there enough for all of us?"

She counted with two nods. "There is, but Butcher won't be happy."

"Butcher's never happy."

I wondered who this Butcher was. It was an odd name. But I didn't have to wait for long.

An old husky pawed into the room. He used the woman as a shield, his bright blue eyes peeking between her legs.

"He's the biggest chicken I've ever seen," Jack said. "And I've raised chickens."

"Dad, I think maybe an introduction is in order."

"Right," Jack said. "Of course. Folks, this is Becca, my wife. Becca, this is my son Dave and his lady friend, whose name has slipped into the ether along with my high school algebra."

"Constance," Other Dave reminded him.

"And she's not the lady you married, right?"

"No. No, she's not." Dave's eyes fell to the floor.

"Right. There I go making an ass of myself again. Constance, I'm sorry I forgot your name. I won't let it happen again, Constance. It *is* Constance, right?"

"It is." I laughed.

"And y'all are staying for dinner, right? We insist."

"Yes, Dad. We're staying for dinner."

30

DAVE'S FATHER

The stew was delicious. There was also nothing for Butcher to worry about. I noticed both Becca and Jack sneak the dog several bites.

Jack opened a bottle of wine, and we retreated from the dining table to the living room with its warm and cozy fire, where Becca got out the ingredients for s'mores.

The girls would've loved to be here with us, and after getting to know Jack a little, I was sure he'd love to meet them too.

On the other hand, Other Dave had yet to get comfortable. After explaining his own predicament, he peppered his father with questions.

"So, you really managed it then... you merged?"

Jack chuckled. "You make it sound like it's a terrible thing—like we're two different species."

"Me and this other guy in my head right now—I think, maybe, we're just that."

"You're not," Jack said loudly. "I know you. I know him. I know you never thought of yourself as just the wolf. You're more than that, son, and you always have been. Even when you were just the wolf."

"Yeah, tell your *other* son that."

"Show him," Jack said. "Show him who you really are and who you can be."

"How?"

"I can't do it for you," Jack said.

"Then how did you do it? How did you merge?"

"Everyone's path is different. All I can say is it was a long and arduous process. And trust was the first step. I was never a hundred percent sure I could trust my other guy. It didn't help the other guy hated my guts. Sound familiar?"

"Very."

"Can I ask something?" I'd been biding my time, hoping to get my question in edgewise.

They nodded.

"How did you two speak before—when you were the wolves?"

Dave had never told me werewolves interacted with each other. I knew they couldn't speak.

"You think witches are the only ones with telepathy?" Jack asked.

"I, uh, well, now I'm not so sure."

Jack's beard bristled with a smile. "Magic flows in us like it does in you. The difference is subtle. We're connected by our bloodline. We can only communicate with our kin, plus anyone we've turned and anyone we've imprinted on."

"Oh."

"And I mean anyone."

"Right."

I had no clue what that comment meant.

But I did know it meant Dave had never imprinted on me. Not that I was sure I wanted him to.

Jack turned his attention back to his son. "A friend of mine, Yancy—someone I'd love for you to meet by the way —he taught me how to let the other guy free for a while. Over some years, we developed a rapport. I started trusting him more and more. He stopped hating me so much. I say I and he, but the truth is now we don't know who is who anymore. We talk and we think so much alike these days."

"Huh." Other Dave scratched at his day-old stubble. "Does that mean you share memories now?"

"It does, but some things got lost in the merge. Some memories."

"Like the night you killed that man?"

"Actually, that's not one of them."

"So, you know then?" Other Dave asked.

His father steepled his fingers. "Yes, I know I never killed anyone."

"That's great, Dad. I'm glad you haven't been living with that on your chest."

"No, just a myriad of other bad decisions."

The wine had taken the wheel. I couldn't hold back my questions any longer. "What did happen that night?"

"Let's start from where you know," Jack answered. "Human me woke up next to a torn up and bloody body. I was sure I'd killed this man. That he must've been out hunting in the wrong woods at the wrong time."

"And?" Like a kid, I smashed a marshmallow between two strips of cracker.

"And that couldn't be further from the truth."

"What do you mean?" Other Dave asked.

"Well, now we're talking about my other memories. My wolf found this guy propped up next to a tree. We knew something was wrong. He wasn't dead yet. He was bleeding bad. But it didn't matter. We'd already feasted on a deer and had no desire to take anything from him."

"So what'd you do?"

"A part of us thought we could save him. So, we licked him, hoping and praying the curse might take hold. Hoping that he'd transform into a wolf like us. Then something else took hold. Some sort of magic I'd never experienced before and never have again. And I just couldn't. I couldn't save him."

"You licked him?" Other Dave questioned.

"I know. That's not how the curse works. I just... I just couldn't."

"Couldn't what?"

They looked at me like I had chocolate on my face. Then I realized I probably did.

It was Becca who spoke. "We hunt for food. We don't kill just to kill. It's not like the movies. But to answer the question, there has to be a bite. And bites aren't something you dole out willingly. Our magic is as complex as any other. As complex as your witch magic. Yes, I could tell as soon as I saw you."

"So the magic told you not to do it?"

"The way I see it, the moon chooses the wolf. This man wasn't chosen."

"And what about the next morning?" Other Dave asked in what sounded a lot like Dave's voice. "Do you remember what you made me do?"

"I remember." Jack pulled a long sip of wine. "That was wrong of me, son. So very wrong. There's so much to apologize for... to... to both of you."

I knew he wasn't talking to me but instead to both versions of Dave.

31

CONSTANCE CAMPBELL AND THE MIDNIGHT MATE

I t was decided that we'd take the spare bedroom. Given the size of the cabin, I thought we were lucky they had one.

What was up in the air—literally—was how we were supposed to get back home. Gavin didn't answer any of our calls the next day.

Jack and Becca showed us around the small town. They took us bowling, introduced us to their werewolf friends, and we rented a movie the next night from Fetch's Flicks.

Nostalgia flooded my veins with the same high I got every Friday night in high school—when renting movies was the thing to do.

The selection was limited but decent. Other Dave made the mistake of letting me pick, and he didn't groan when I took *10 Things I Hate About You* up to the cash register.

We watched this classic film with another bottle of wine and a lot more s'mores.

I hated to say I was enjoying the company. Although, it meant sharing a bed with him at night. I kept reminding myself the real Dave was in there too.

I lined pillows between us in bed. Not that it mattered. We were still in layers of thermal underwear and pajamas. The chill of outside penetrated the cabin walls with ease.

Other Dave stretched out on the other side of Fort Pillows, his head atop his outstretched hands. "I'll try Gavin again tomorrow."

"Okay," I said. "What happens if you don't reach him?"

"I was giving that some thought. I think I might know someone who could help."

"Really? Who?"

"This, uh, demon fellow. Custos or something. I meant to tell you the other day. He's taken up residence at your Gran's place."

"I knew it smelled the other day. You really weren't going to tell me unless it was necessary?"

"He asked me to give him a few days to clear out."

"So, you two are pals?"

"Not exactly. He was a little mad I ruined his fun."

"That was him at Orange Blossoms?" I shook my head. "No good deed goes unpunished."

"If you summon him here, he can take us back."

"It's slightly more complicated than that, but yes, he should be able to."

"What's the complication?"

"Demons like to trade in favors. And his favors have already cost me a lot."

I WOKE to the press of a warm body against my back. A hard body, in more ways than one.

As much as Dave wanted to pretend his muscles were built on something more than his wolfish nature, I knew better. The man spent as much time in the gym as I did drinking tea over coffee.

Dave didn't need to pump up his chest, back, or arms. They were already knotted with lean muscle. Often, I'd caught myself staring as he stepped out of the shower, his back bare in all its sinewy glory.

Except this wasn't the real Dave.

He wrapped a heavy arm around my waist and tugged me closer.

His warmth radiated over the entire bed. I wondered where the wall of pillows had gone.

I rolled over, my eyes heavy with sleep. I blinked them open and struggled to see more than his silhouette in the darkness. With my palm, I could feel the smattering of dark hair across his chest.

Slowly, my eyes adjusted to the lack of light. It was dark most of the day anyway. A thin beam of moonlight peeked through the window shades. With it, I made out Dave's dark eyes.

Other Dave.

His eyes were open and focused on me. Intense, but not necessarily in a bad way.

"Hi," I said.

"Hi," he said. "I didn't mean to wake you."

I combed my fingers through his hair. "Are you both awake?"

"We are."

Other Dave nestled against my neck, his breath hot, giving me goosebumps.

Now, I was truly awake. My insides fluttered as he pressed his lips against my skin. He kissed my hair, my ear, my neck.

Those lips were so soft, a sharp contrast to the ever-present stubble on his chin.

I didn't mind it, not as his kisses plunged lower, grazing my collarbone. But when those kisses dipped lower to my chest, I knew I had to put a stop to it.

"We can't," I said.

"Can't or won't? Or you don't want to?"

"I don't know. It's complicated."

"Because I'm not really your boyfriend?"

"Something like that."

Other Dave let out a low growl.

I was tempted to do the same.

Why did magic have to be so... so annoying. I wanted this. I wanted him.

Except I didn't know what I wanted anymore. Who I wanted.

The real Dave?

But did the real Dave want me?

What about this wolfish version? Did he love me?

And what did it say about me if I wanted him to?

32

POLICE WORK

OTHER DAVE

The return journey was as unsettling as unsettling gets. Getting hauled off through the shadow realm. The demon could've easily shipped us off to some netherworld and stashed us away forever.

But he didn't.

He was true to his word.

We were back in Creel Creek well before the arrival of the full moon. The problem was, I wasn't happy about being back.

Something about Constance had changed in the last few days.

Back here, things reverted to the way they were before.

She sent me packing.

I filled the next day with police work, of all things. That and I wanted to nail Maude for what she'd done to my father. I wanted to catch this other culprit too.

It helped to occupy my mind.

Except a part of my mind refused to be occupied.

You love her, Dave said.

"So what? You love her too. *I know you do.*"

Your point?

"What's been stopping you?"

I... I don't know.

33

THE ROOMMATE PACT

As expected, Custos required a favor to transport us home safely. But it wasn't nearly as big or earth shattering as the first I'd granted him—letting him loose from the underworld for a day. Mother Gaia had already worked out a more permanent deal in that regard.

His ask was simple—to extend his stay at Gran's house for an uncertain length of time. Since Gran's stay with Mother Gaia was also uncertain, I didn't see any harm allowing it. If he cleaned up his own messes and didn't have any crazy parties with his otherworldly friends, things would work out fine.

We hadn't been back in Creel Creek for ten minutes before Gavin returned Other Dave's calls.

Too little. Too late.

We wouldn't be using his services again. Although I could see more visits up to Canada in our future. That was, of course, if my Dave felt the same way as his wolfish counterpart about his father and his new stepmother.

Becca had been nothing but sweet, and Jack had blown my picture of him out of the water with his sincerity and kindness. Maybe the merge had been what he'd needed all along.

In total, we'd been gone for a few days. There was plenty of time for Other Dave to prepare for his monthly transition... if it happened.

I couldn't help wondering what would happen if their roles continued to be reversed. What if this time, the wolf turned out to be Dave.

My Dave.

It was almost worth venturing to the mountain to find out.

Not that either Dave would allow me to do that.

I spent that night at Dave's with Mom and the girls. Other Dave spent the night before the full moon at Gran's house with Brad, Stevie, and Custos.

The demon couldn't comprehend the trouble he'd gotten himself into with his shenanigans over the last month. I was biding my time, and his, by waiting to tell Trish and the other witches in person who their not-quite-lover had been.

After a nice long chat with Mom, I settled in our king-sized bed alone. Sleep didn't come easy. I was restless. I missed the comfort of Dave's warm body beside me.

But which Dave did I want?

Maybe both.

My alarm sounded early the next morning. It felt as if I'd just gotten to sleep, which was probably more accurate than I wanted to believe.

The drive to work was uneventful, and so were the first few hours. I was glad to see an uptick in customers as the whole Tyson Briggs situation blew over.

Creel Creek was back to its usual eerie self.

But only half of the mystery was solved. We knew

without a shadow of a doubt that Maude had played a role in her husband's death.

Knowing and proving are two separate things.

We still didn't understand how she'd done it.

As far as I knew, Mac was no closer to solving Tyson's case either.

The problem is, when a case goes cold, there usually has to be an introduction of new evidence or a new witness to reignite it.

Until then, it's a waiting game.

I wasn't waiting too long, just nearing the end of my shift, when a woman in scrubs cozied up to the counter. The nurse from Creel Creek Commons, the assisted living facility, smiled up at me. "Hello again."

"Oh, hi." I smiled. "It's Jennifer, right?"

I smacked my own forehead, realizing a second later she was wearing her name tag.

"That's right." She laughed. "This is actually my first time in. This place is gorgeous. What do you recommend?"

"Our signature lattes are popular." I pointed up at the menu.

"Yeah. That looks good. I'll get two of those Charmed Caramel Lattes. To go, please."

"Two?" I questioned. "I guess that means you're working tonight?"

"I am," she groaned. "But the extra latte's not for me. I promised my roommate I'd pick her up something for when I see her at work. She hates when we trade shifts. Says it ruins her sleep cycle. Not that I love it either, but I had a few things I had to get done today."

I nodded in understanding. "That's the thing about working nine to five. If you need to get business done during the day, you have to miss work."

"Right? It's so dumb. Like why doesn't the DMV have a night shift?"

"Can you imagine how slow it would be?" I laughed.

"So slow. But better than a day off for a new license photo."

She made a good point.

I reached for some to-go cups and jotted her name down on the side of the first cup.

"What's your roommate's name?" I asked.

"Emily," she said. "Although sometimes she likes to go by Ginger Snaps. So, either is fine."

The Sharpie in my hand made a not-so-sharp scribble down the side of the cup.

"Emily," I repeated. "As in Maude's favorite nurse? Y'all are roommates."

"One and the same."

"And she's *not* working tonight?"

"No, ma'am. Maude's going to be thrilled to see me, I'm sure."

My mind was whirling.

It was more than a coincidence. Much more. I'd been so quick to cross Ginger and New Moon off my suspect list.

This was the new information the case needed.

Maude must've told Emily how she got away with her husband's murder. She'd probably given her some set of instructions that Emily had carried out on Tyson.

I had to figure out what those instructions were. I told Trish as much when she came to the cafe to relieve me.

"Did you tell Dave?" she asked.

"A. It's not really Dave. B. He's wolfing out tonight. And C. He might not shift."

"And I thought my love life was complicated." Trish ran

a hand through her hair. It fell in chunky strands across her face.

"Yeah, let's talk about that when I get back."

"You're going there? Tonight? Without Dave?"

"He and Allie should be leaving for their campsite any minute now."

"Maybe you should call Mac?"

"He doesn't know much about this case. Besides, I don't think I have much to worry about from an elderly lady. It's not like she's responsible for Tyson's death."

"From what you've told me, she kind of is. And she's definitely responsible for her husband's..."

"She's old. I have magic. Magic I plan to use to interrogate her."

"What does that mean? You're going to magically waterboard her?" Trish blew a purple streak of hair from over her green eyes.

"I'm going to say please," I told her, hoping the same magical trick would work twice.

"You're desperate. You know, normally I'd try to talk you out of this."

"But not this time?"

"No point," she said. "It's never worked before. I do expect a phone call by sundown."

"A phone call, really?"

"Or a text. If I don't get one, I'm calling the posse and we're rounding you up."

"Fair enough."

I took off my apron, scooped my purse from behind the counter, and left. All the while, Trish's eyes bore daggers in the back of my head.

It wasn't good to get on her bad side.

TRISH REALLY HADN'T GIVEN me much time. The sun was working its way over the mountains in the west.

While Prongs made the drive across town in record time, I didn't have long before I was supposed to send Trish a text with an "All Clear."

I typed it out but didn't hit send.

The lady at the reception desk told me I had to be quick, that visiting hours were over in fifteen minutes. So, I promised I would be. I signed in, then retraced the route to Maude's room.

There was no sign of Jennifer at the nurse's station, but I saw her coffee cup sitting beside a computer monitor.

Where before, I thought the residents exuded a need for company, now, the whole place came across as uninviting. The atmosphere was staler than before, the lighting too bright.

For the most part, the halls of Creel Creek Commons were eerily quiet. My sneakers squeaked on the recently mopped floor. I heard the drone of televisions coming from a few rooms. Other doors were open to darkness within.

None of the residents were roaming around by themselves either.

I rapped lightly on Maude's door, afraid she might already be asleep.

Her raspy voice beckoned me inside almost immediately. "Come in," she said. "Is that you, Emily?"

Like the other room I'd passed, her room was dark inside. Maude was alone in her bed, the covers wrapped tightly, up close to her neck. I couldn't see much else.

I wanted to turn on a lamp or something. The closest

option was the fluorescent light above our heads, which I opted against.

Too bright.

"I believe Emily's off tonight." I inched inside the room.

"That's right," she said weakly.

"Maude" —I inched closer— "do you remember me?"

She leaned forward, her eyes narrowing, before she came to an abrupt stop. She hiccupped a tiny laugh. "I thought you might come."

The elderly woman fell back onto her pillows.

That was when I noticed the straps, some snaking beneath the blankets to her ankles, the others to her wrists.

She was tied down to the bed.

My immediate desire was to free her and to come down on her nurses for treating her this way.

A familiar prickle on my neck warned against it. The urge died away almost as quickly as it had come.

"What do you mean?" I asked. "Why would you think that?"

"A feeling," she rasped. "That and you had your eye on my bracelet."

"I don't even remember your bracelet," I said.

"It's just there, on the dresser. You can bring it to me if you like."

My eyes caught the hint of silver on her dresser. But that same prickle on my neck told me not to touch it.

"Maude, why are you tied up?"

"They have to do it," she said. "I do strange things at the full moon. It's for their own protection. And mine. Otherwise, I hurt people. Now... bring me the bracelet!" Her voice went rabid with rage.

I ignored her like she was a five-year-old having a tantrum. "Was Emily here... the night of the last full moon?"

"She was." Maude shook violently against her restraints. "But Jennifer took my bracelet that night. I saw her do it."

I'd been wrong.

I'd been played.

"Where is Jennifer now?" I asked.

A different sensation on my neck gave me the answer, an answer I didn't want. The sharp pinch of a needle jabbed into my skin.

"Behind you." Jennifer's voice combined with the squeeze of the needle sent chills down my spine.

I'd watched enough suspense movies to know what happens when you let your guard down, allowing the bad guy to sneak up behind you.

Unlike the defenseless main characters in those movies, I had magic.

Or did I?

Weirdly, I couldn't feel the flow of it in my veins.

I felt... nothing.

"It doesn't matter if you scream," Jennifer said. "We're used to screams coming from this room."

"What have you done?" I asked her.

"Nothing yet. Not to you."

But that couldn't be true. Where was my magic?

With her other hand in my back, she forced me closer to Maude's bed.

"Now, Maude," she said. "I'm going to give you your medicine a little early tonight. I have a few things to take care of. Will you be okay here, on your own?"

"She wouldn't give me my bracelet," Maude screamed.

"Constance." Jennifer grinned. "You're smarter than I thought."

"What's wrong with her?" I asked. "What does the bracelet do?"

"I thought you were good at this kind of thing?" She shook her head with a tsk. "Maude's family's lineage had the curse of a werewolf until some witch lifted it. Come on. I bet you know whose lineage that witch was from, don't you?"

"Mine."

"I knew you'd be a good guesser." Her smile was wicked. "This witch thought she'd done them a kindness. She was wrong. So wrong. Maude's family still changes at the full moon. They just don't become beasts. Isn't that right... Grandma?"

"My daughter never visits," Maude said.

"She's right," Jennifer said. "Mom's not really a fan of hers."

With her free hand, Jennifer pulled another syringe from her back pocket. She stuck this one in an IV port attached to Maude, then plunged it down.

Maude fell silent.

Satisfied, Jennifer snatched the bracelet off the dresser. "It took me a while to track this thing down. Someone stole it from her at some point, probably not too long after she used it."

"What is it?" I asked, although now I sensed the magical energy emanating from it.

"A devious invention from a warlock—at least that's what she told me. From what I understand, he's been operating around here nearly as long as your family has."

Ivan.

Jennifer held up the bracelet, its moon and stars charms dangling. "This baby turns its wearer into a faux wolf of sorts. That is, if they have the affliction like Maude here... or me."

She pocketed it.

"I don't think I'll need it tonight though. Not when we

can have the *real* thing. It's nearly an hour before the moon rises. Best we get prepared."

"For what?"

"I, no we, have plans tonight."

"No." I went to shake my head but was reminded Jennifer had a syringe jabbed into my neck. "Why did you kill Tyson?"

"Like everything in life," she said. "It's complicated. Why did Grandma kill Grandpa? Again, it's complicated."

This was about as crazy as it gets.

I needed magic, and I needed it now. It didn't matter if I couldn't feel it, I was going to whisper a spell anyway when Jennifer plunged the contents of the syringe down hard. The icy chill of the syringe's contents snaked into my veins, then the whole world went black.

34

CONSTANCE CAMPBELL AND THE
HOWL AT THE MOON

I came to in what looked like a mostly empty barn. An oil lamp hung near the door, lighting most of the space and casting large shadows over others.

The floor beneath my body was wooden and caked in cold but dry dirt. There were cobwebs on the rafters of the ceiling. An old tractor in the corner was half concealed by a tattered covering with its large front wheel exposed. Its shadow made a tall monster on the back, where a few pieces of farming equipment hung—a rake, a spade, and a scythe.

A sense of sheer dread weighted me to the floor. But that wasn't the only thing. My head was pounding. My arms and my legs were heavier than I remembered and hard to move.

I couldn't get up if I wanted to. And as my last few memories caught up with me, I wanted to.

I wanted to run. To get away.

Frantically, my eyes searched the room for Jennifer but didn't find her anywhere. I patted my pockets, looking for my phone, but didn't find it.

Sounds outside the barn captured my attention. A

tractor or an ATV came to a stop. Then footsteps scuffed their way into the barn with me.

A figure stepped between me and the lamp light. This time, instead of a syringe, Jennifer held a gun. "About time you woke up."

"What do you want?" I asked.

"I want you to get up. Let's get going. It's almost time."

When I failed to respond, she kicked me in the ribs. "Up! Now!"

"Or what?"

"Or I shoot you. Isn't that obvious?"

"You won't get away this." It was the most cliché thing, but it was all my brain could put together.

"Does that mean you think your friends are on the way?" She laughed. "Thanks for typing out that text for me. When I used your face to open your phone, I just went ahead and hit send. I hope that's okay?"

I didn't answer. If there was no Trish on her way, then I was truly helpless.

And somehow without magic.

"Come on." She kicked me again.

"You know that's counterproductive, right?"

With a great effort, I stood and wobbled forward. Using the barrel of her shotgun, Jennifer shoved me sideways. "Keep moving or else you'll fall again. We don't want that."

Outside the barn, there was an ATV. It had a trailer hitched to the back of it with what could be described as a cage of some sort on top.

"Is that for me?" Not that I was planning on stepping a foot inside it. She could shoot me first.

"That's for my protection," she said coolly. "Now, go."

"Go? Go where?"

I was already mid escape plan, trying to get the lay of the

land around us, looking for an easy path away from Jennifer and, more importantly, her gun.

But my brain was too fuzzy to put together the pieces.

We were in the middle of farmland. It was too dark out to see much of anything. There was a pasture, and a creek trickled through the middle of it. I could just make out a fence at the edge of the property. Behind it, there was nothing but woods... and a mountain.

She pressed the butt of the gun into my chest and nudged me through the high grass of the pasture.

There wasn't a cow or horse in sight.

"It's almost the full moon," I pointed out, searching the sky for what, I didn't know.

"I'm aware," she said. "We have about five minutes to get you close."

"Close to what?" I asked.

"To Emily." She shoved me again. "Go ahead. She's out there waiting for you. That coffee was perfect, by the way. Although, Em thought it tasted a little bitter. Probably because of those sleeping pills I added."

Emily?

"How is Emily involved?"

"She isn't involved, you idiot. She's the victim. It's perfect. She loves werewolves so much. She's like their number one fan. Now she gets to be mauled by one."

"You realize this makes no sense, right?"

"You're on drugs," she countered. "None of it's going to make much sense to you."

Jennifer kept stepping forward. I kept stepping backward. The gun had created a tender spot in my back. I didn't want another push.

I didn't mind heading up the mountain toward Emily. With her help, maybe we could both escape.

"Why Emily?" I asked her.

"Because Emily took Tyson away."

"No. You killed Tyson."

"I said she took him away, not that *she* killed him." She jogged up and smacked the tender spot with the butt of the gun. It sent me to my knees. "Get up."

"How?"

"With your legs."

"No." I struggled to my feet. "How did she take Tyson away?"

"We're roommates," Jennifer said. "We share a lot of things."

"You shared Tyson?"

"Gross. No. Emily had me post messages for their little group when she was at work. Then I found their private messages and one thing led to another…"

Creepy.

"Don't judge me," she snapped. "Tyson knew I wasn't the real Ginger Snaps. It's not like we were in love. He told me what they were up to—what they were going to do. They were going to use my cage like it was for diving with deadly sharks. They wanted to observe the werewolf from it. Can you believe that? Well, I'm sure you can. They wanted to move it up the mountain and spend the night inside it, waiting for a werewolf to show up."

"Did Emily know what you really used it for?"

"No," Jennifer said. "I told her my father had used it for trapping live animals."

"But it was really for you," I said. "When you were your Hyde."

"Don't call it that," she snapped. "When Tyson came snooping around, they'd locked him inside it. Tried to scare him into believing. But then they chickened out. They set him free. But he was still hanging around the house when I came home to make my change."

"What happened that night?"

"I gave Grandma a sedative, just like I always do. I came home. I got in the cage. I locked myself in, like I always do. And then—"

"Tyson came into the barn," I finished.

She nodded. "He thought they'd locked me up as another joke. He didn't understand that I was already in a rage. A fit. I was so angry. He found the key and unlocked the cage. I had the bracelet in my pocket."

"And you put it on?"

"It wasn't the real me who made that choice," she said. "I didn't mean to kill him."

"But you mean to kill Emily," I said.

"It's you who's going to kill Emily."

"Yeah, I still don't get that."

"I know what you are," she said. "I knew it as soon as I saw you."

It wasn't the first time I'd been found out. Her knowing I was a witch didn't faze me. The twisted grin on her face, however, made me question everything. "What exactly do you think I am?"

"A werewolf." She was serious.

I would've snorted a laugh, but there was a gun pointed at my chest.

"I knew the sheriff couldn't be the only one, not in a town teeming with paranormals. Even if he were, it didn't matter."

"Why's that?" I asked.

"He was sure to have the same problem his father had all those years ago. Because I left the scene in the same way. He would either have to bury the body—and bury any evidence with it. Or he was going to take the blame. Then I saw you, and I knew I was off the hook."

"What makes you think I'm a werewolf?"

"I saw you," she repeated. "I saw you running up the mountain like an injured fawn. So petite. Nothing like the big bad wolf I'd pictured."

She'd seen Allie.

"I waited for morning. You'd curled up into a tarp near the hunting blind. So, I made the scene near it."

"Why so close to your grandfather's body?"

"That was just a weird coincidence. I didn't know where his body was hidden." She shrugged and checked her watch. "Two minutes. Keep walking."

"You know I'm not really a werewolf," I told her.

"Exactly what a werewolf would say." She checked her watch again. "Another minute or so, and we'll find out. Besides, I've got to get back to the farm before I—"

A sudden sense of magic began building deep within my chest.

It was back. I was back. I could fight. I could take the gun away.

And I could do so much more.

I smiled.

"Don't get any ideas," she warned. "There are silver slugs in here. Real silver. Not that sterling crap your boyfriend got shot with. You're probably wishing he was here to help you right now."

That was it.

No more Miss Nice Witch.

Magic built, surging from my spine through my arms, hands, and fingertips.

I readied a spell on my lips as the alarm on Jennifer's watch began to ping.

It was time to act. I started to wave my hand but found there wasn't a hand there to wave. In its place was something that looked a whole lot like a paw.

Curse at the Moon, the Moon curses back, a voice, oddly reminiscent of my own, whispered in the back of my mind.

"I knew it," Jennifer yelled. She aimed the shotgun at me, with it silver slugs. "I knew you were a wolf."

I closed my eyes, sure she was about to take a shot.

Nothing happened.

When I opened my eyes again, Jennifer's features had changed. Her eyes had gone wide with rage. Her mouth twisted into a sneer.

With a roar, she threw the shotgun into the tall grass beside us. I expected her to run—run up to the farm and lock herself in the cage. That was what it was there for.

Apparently, that ship had sailed.

She roared again, then dug a hand inside the pocket of her scrubs, finding the bracelet and holding it up in triumph.

I don't think we want her to put that on, the voice said.

The voice was right. I lunged at Jennifer, but it was already too late. She was morphing—changing into something out of a cold-blooded killer's nightmare.

Her flesh took on a metallic gleam. Her torso expanded in height and width. Long, thick arms hung from wide shoulders. What scared me most were the large blades at the ends of them.

Who does she think she is—Wolverine?

Maybe you want to run? the voice inside my head suggested.

Good idea!

I turned tail and ran for the woods. Jennifer was in hot pursuit.

Are you like my inner wolf? I asked.

Not quite. I'm more like a manifestation of your magic talking.

That's a thing?

It is now. You really pissed off the Moon, huh?

I didn't mean to.

Well, we're in this together now. Let's try to come out of it alive.

Getting out alive sounded good. But there were obstacles.

My wolf form was fast. Powerful. The good thing was I had my mind. And my magic.

Wait, I thought. *Can't you do something? Can we perform a spell?*

I... I don't think so. Your magic—it's doing this.

It made me a werewolf.

We raced up the mountain, the metallic monster behind me snarling and snapping its metal jaws, which scraped together like clashing swords.

"What's the matter, Constance?" Her voice had a tinny quality. "Wolf got your tongue? Are you scared because I'm made of silver?"

Not good.

Run faster, the magic encouraged.

The problem was we were running the wrong way. I smelled something. Someone.

Emily.

She wasn't safe. Not out here with Jennifer's beast.

There was a howl in the distance. Another wolf. They weren't safe either. Jennifer could kill Dave and Allie. She could kill Emily, and me too.

Dave! I tried shouting, but it too came out as a howl, a howl at the Moon.

Can he hear me? Can he understand?

He could be on the other side of the mountain for all I knew.

"I hear you, Constance." Dave's voice was unlike any other thing in my mind. It wasn't like the booming echo of a familiar. And not like the whisper of my magic. It was both soothing and reassuring, just like his touch.

I'd stopped a moment to let out the howl, longer after hearing Dave's voice.

It was a moment too long. A blade sliced my side, sending a shooting pain across my whole body.

Dave, I thought again. But this time, I was in agony.

My body reacted on instinct. I dodged her next assault, and I lashed out, connecting a paw to her face.

"We hear you." It was Other Dave's voice, and it had that same soothing quality. "Keep coming this way."

But... but she's made of steel?

"It's okay," they said. "You aren't a werewolf. Not really. Silver isn't going to kill you like it would us."

But the blades still hurt, I argued.

"Then fight back," Dave encouraged. "And keep coming up the mountain."

Jennifer swiped at me. I ducked below it. Reaching out, my claws connected with her neck, glancing off the metal.

What about Emily?

"She's safe."

How? How are you talking to me?

"We, uh, we figured some things out too," Dave said. "We haven't merged or anything crazy. But we're working together now."

He's imprinted on you, my magic said with a note of sass.

Okay, I thought. *But how is Emily safe?*

"We had a sit-down with Mac earlier," Dave said.

"There's a fox shifter up here holding a pair of handcuffs. Just fight back."

I'm trying.

Jennifer climbed a rock and leaped, her claws slashing wildly through the air. I ducked in the nick of time, dipping away from her and connecting my own claws to her shin. They bounced off the metal.

I ran forward only for Jennifer to mount another attack. I dove out of the way.

The funny thing was I didn't seem to lose any energy. If anything, the chase had given me more.

But how was I supposed to overcome an object made of metal?

Jennifer snarled. She ran at me again. Those metal claws aimed straight into my chest.

Out of the corner of my eye, I saw something—the dangle of a charm at her wrist.

I dodged her attack one last time. Reached out the tip of my claw, and it came away with the bracelet. In mid-air, Jennifer morphed again. Her human body thumped to the ground with a loud thud.

Finally, it was over, but with one big exception.

I was still a werewolf.

35

GODDESSES

S pending the rest of the night as a wolf wasn't my favorite thing. But it didn't seem like I or my magic had much of a choice.

I watched, horrified, as Dave taught Allie how to take down a deer. Then, to my utmost horror, I had a strong inclination to partake in the meal that followed.

Yuck.

I won't even discuss how awkward the trip home the next morning was. Dave and Allie both had changes of clothes. I stole Dave's boxers, his uniform jacket, and wrapped myself in a blanket he kept in the back of the SUV.

We returned to Dave's house where Mom treated us to a proper breakfast of blueberry pancakes.

The next week was a blur. Mac and Dave got the evidence they needed. Maude and Jennifer were sent to a place where they'd be caged twenty-four seven.

And for the next little while, all was right with the world.

Except something kept bothering me. How had the scene been so close to the *other* body? Was it really a coincidence?

Was it me—was my magic to blame?

Maybe.

Maybe the shifters were right. I was connected to Dave's moon curse. After all, it was the find of the older body that set certain things in motion—Other Dave's reconnection with his father, Dave's reconciliation with his *other* half, and my connection to them as well.

I pondered these things as I parked at Gran's house, traipsed through the back yard, and found the familiar path through the woods.

Not all witches work spells in graveyards. Not all witches perform them at midnight under the crescent moon. But those who do find these spells perform better than others done any other time or in any other way.

The magic's always there for us. It's up to us to harness it. And a graveyard, under the crescent moon at the witching hour, is the best way to do so.

I waited for the others where the trail spit out to the clearing. Trish, Lauren, and Kalene filed into the clearing. Summer, along with Mom, made us six in total.

Above us, the moon was mostly cloaked in the Earth's shadow. All of it except a golden sliver that hung low like a crooked smile.

We walked up the hill together, put our palms against the old oak, and we asked Mother Gaia for guidance and answers.

At my turn, we were caught off guard by the hoot of an owl. Everyone craned their necks to catch sight of it, perched along a jagged branch about halfway up the tree.

It was rare to see an animal inside the graveyard. There were never any squirrels. I'd never seen a mouse or any other rodent.

This particular owl had been here before—when Other Dave caught me here trying to spell him away.

Why it was here now begged many questions.

That was until it swooped down from its perch, landing in the form of a woman. An older woman. About my height. With a sturdy build.

"Gran?"

"You didn't think I'd be gone forever, did you?"

"What were you doing as an owl?"

"I had a task to complete," she said. "Given to me by a goddess herself."

"The Moon," several of us answered.

She smirked. "Nothing gets by you lot."

"Not exactly true," Trish argued.

Lauren tried wrapping an arm around her friend's shoulder, and Trish shuddered away. Lauren was left embracing Summer and Kalene instead.

Gran wasn't there for tender moments. She trudged down the hill with me chasing after.

"That was you—you who cursed Dave?"

"My magic did," she said. "But it was the Moon who wanted it done?"

"And you made me trust the other Dave?"

"Your magic did that, my dear."

"Right."

"So, this is it—this is how you're going to return? You don't want to tell us what it was like? What happened with the Mother?"

"She reconnected with her sister. I'll leave it at that, for now." Gran made long strides through the clearing. "That and I'm ready to get home. I think I'll have a bath and sleep for a week straight. They work long hours, the goddesses do."

"Your house?" I sucked in a breath. "You're sure you don't want to visit with me and Mom? She'd love to see you."

"Don't tell lies," Gran spat. "I told you, I'm tired, and I'm ready to be home after a long time away. There's nothing you could do or say that'd stop me from wanting that."

"True," I lied.

Gran disappeared down the path.

36

CREEL CREEK AFTER DARK

SEASON 3: EPISODE 14

It's getting late.
So very late.
You hear something go bump in the night.
Are you afraid?
You should be!
Welcome to Creel Creek After Dark.

Athena: Good evening, folks. I'm your host, Athena Hunter.

Ivana: I'm her cohost, Ivana Steak.

Athena: And in case you've forgotten since the intro, this is *Creel Creek After Dark*.

Ivana: Funny you should mention forgetting, Athena. You know… I, myself, lost my memory for several months without any suitable explanation from any doctor.

Athena: Ivana—we've been over this.

Ivana: I'm not backing down this time—because I think you know something.

Athena: Ivana, I…

Ivana: I already know. You don't have an explanation.

But it wasn't like I was hit over the head. I didn't wake up bedridden in a coma. I woke up at a party—a wake for some man I'd never met. A former cohost of this very show.

Athena: We've talked about this before.

Ivana: And we can go over it a thousand more times. I won't stop until I'm satisfied. Change of plans. That's exactly what I'd like for tonight's show. Let's go over this one last time. And this time in front of a live virtual audience. So, there's nowhere for you to run, Athena. You can't wave your hands and try to force the past away.

Athena: I have nothing to hide.

Ivana: So here it is, folks. Season Two: The Lost Episode. Because I want answers.

Athena: If you want answers, Ivana, you're going to have to ask some questions.

Ivana: I can do that. Here's the first. I want to know who exactly was Ivan Rush? And, what I'd really like to know is why he keeps showing up in my dreams...

37

EPILOGUE

Dave cranked the car and turned down the stereo, which had been blaring *Jessie's Girl* by Rick Springfield.

"Sorry," he said. "I was introducing Other Dave to Eighties rock."

"I like that song," I said and turned the dial up again.

Dave jammed out, playing percussion on the steering wheel, but that wasn't all he was doing with his hands.

I noticed he kept tapping on the inside of his coat pocket. It looked almost like he was checking if something was still there.

When he caught me looking, he quickly went back to his dashboard drum set, crashing the invisible cymbals and doing a drumroll on the horn.

He accidentally beeped it at the car in front of us. "Oops."

When we parked, he made another move for the pocket, groping at the bulge in his chest, then adjusting it so it was hardly noticeable.

Dave buttoned two of the three buttons, and it struck

me how much the addition of a jacket did to his usual look. He was handsome all the time. On our date nights, he usually wore a nice shirt, dark jeans, boots, and never a tie.

The jacket was the icing on a delectable Dave-shaped cake. It made his shoulders broader and his chest more pronounced.

But what is that bulge?

There was no one inside my mind to answer my questions anymore.

We went in. It was the same ole Orange Blossoms, if a little more subdued than the last time.

I doubted tonight would have as many fireworks. No demon parading around as multiple people.

Yet, to my surprise, the booths *were* filled with people I knew. Trish, Lauren, and Summer were sharing a meal together, as if that was something normal for them.

Maybe they were commiserating about Custos—or planning their revenge.

My friend Cyrus was sitting alone at the bar with a glass of wine, and a few of Dave's detectives were cozied up with beers in hand. Mac shot a wink in our general direction.

I even thought I saw Gran.

No way.

The older woman I'd mistaken her for disappeared into the restroom.

We ordered our usual drinks and bread, followed by a meal. All the while, Dave was again preoccupied. Not with his phone or a TV.

He kept checking that pocket.

He put his silverware down and scrubbed a napkin across his chin. "Is it me or does the steak taste better tonight than it has, maybe ever?"

"I have the shrimp." I pointed with a fork down at my plate.

"Right... do you want to try mine?" He stabbed a sliver of steak and offered it across the table.

I waved him off. "I'm fine. Actually, I'm thinking about laying off red meat for a while."

He laughed. "I can't say I blame you. I never asked you what you thought about it."

"About being a werewolf?"

"Yeah." He nodded.

"It was scary. But also kind of cool."

His hand grazed his jacket pocket again. It was becoming a tic. "You know I love you, right? We love you."

"You and *Other* Dave?" I said, smiling.

"He doesn't want to be called that anymore. And I agree."

"But he's there with you... now?"

Dave nodded. "Most of the time."

I smiled. "I love both of you. That is, I love all of you, Dave Marsters."

"And I love all of you too, Constance Campbell."

"All of me? Are you saying I'm—"

"No traps tonight." He smiled.

"I would never." I laughed.

"But would you..."

Dave bent down on a knee, and he reached inside the same pocket he'd been grasping at the entire night.

THAT NIGHT, Dave was like a man possessed.

It was like he needed something, and that something was me.

I tried to recall what he'd said about changing into the wolf—what it felt like when his *other* side took over.

"It feels like a release," he'd said.

Maybe he needed that release.

And I did too.

We both took what we wanted.

I wanted him. My Dave. Wolf Dave. All of him.

This wasn't our first time. Far from it. But there was something about it—something new.

Thank you for reading *What Witches Want: Book 7 in the Witching Hour series*. We'd love if you left a review!

For more Witching Fun, be sure to check for the next in series: *There's Something About Magic* or look for other books by Christine Zane Thomas!

ACKNOWLEDGMENTS

Thanks to Paula Lester, who edited this book.

Thanks to Jenn for being my amazing partner in this writing journey.

Thanks to my family. I love all you crazies.

Special thanks to covid, who almost prevented this book from being done on time (again).

ABOUT CHRISTINE ZANE THOMAS

Christine Zane Thomas is the pen name of a husband and wife team. A shared love of mystery and sleuths spurred the creation of their own mysterious writer alter-ego.

While not writing, they can be found in northwest Florida with their two children, their dachshund Queenie, and schnauzer Tinker Bell. When not at home, their love of food takes them all around the South. Sometimes they sprinkle in a trip to Disney World. Food and Wine is their favorite season.

ALSO BY CHRISTINE ZANE THOMAS

Comics and Coffee Case Files starring Kirby Jackson and Gambit

Printed in Great Britain
by Amazon